*Perfect freedom i   *

Summer started her Jet Ski, feeling the unfamiliar vibrations through the soles of her bare feet.

"Better go slow till we're out from under these pilings," Marquez suggested.

Summer grinned. They were going to arrive at the fabulous Merrick estate on roaring Jet Skis like a couple of modern mermaids. Much cooler than showing up on foot, all worn out from the walk.

Summer pressed her throttle button. The Jet Ski seemed to fly, skimming over the surface of the water, hopping from ripple to ripple, sending up a shower of spray in all directions that soon had Summer drenched, hair flying in the hot breeze.

This was why she had come to Crab Claw Key. This very moment. This sense of being in a new place, doing new things with new people. This overpowering, exhilarating feeling of perfect freedom in the middle of a perfect world.

Don't miss the other books in this
romantic series:

#1 June Dreams
#2 July's Promise
#3 August Magic
#4 Sand, Surf, and Secrets
#5 Rays, Romance, and Rivalry
#6 Beaches, Boys, and Betrayal
Special edition Spring Break Reunion

Available from ARCHWAY Paperbacks

Summer

June Dreams

Katherine Applegate

AN ARCHWAY PAPERBACK
Published by POCKET BOOKS
New York   London   Toronto   Sydney   Tokyo   Singapore

For Michael

AN ARCHWAY PAPERBACK *Original*

 An Archway Paperback published by
POCKET BOOKS, a division of Simon & Schuster Inc.
1230 Avenue af the Americas, New York, NY 10020

Produced by Daniel Weiss Associates, Inc., New York

Copyright © 1995 by Daniel Weiss Associates, Inc., and
        Katherine Applegate

ISBN: 0-671-51030-4

First Archway Paperback printing June 1995

10 9 8 7 6 5 4 3 2

AN ARCHWAY PAPERBACK and colophon are
registered trademarks of Simon & Schuster Inc.

Printed in the U.S.A.

IL 7+

1

Bloomington, Minnesota.
February. Not Having a Good Time.

I hate my life. I hate my life. And I hate Sean Valletti."

The school bus had dropped Summer Smith six blocks from her home, and now she had frozen slush in the tops of her boots. Her toes were numb. Her ears were painful. Her lips were chapped. Her face was stiff from the cold and stung by the wind whipping her blond hair. Her gloved fingers, wrapped around her eleventh-grade biology text and a three-ring binder, were weak claws. Her blue eyes streamed tears as she faced into the bitter wind that tore at her, teased her, sneaked through every opening in her clothes to slither along her goose-pimpled flesh.

As for Sean Valletti, she hated him because he was incredibly gorgeous, very mature, and did not know that she existed. Despite the fact that

Summer had often stared longingly at the back of his head in the school lunchroom, despite the fact that she'd sat next to him in biology five days in a row and had even had an actual dream about him, Sean did not know she existed.

And today, as Summer was leaving school after the last bell, he had stopped in the doorway, looked out at the cold, miserable world outside, and said, "Hey, you live near me. Why don't I drive you home in my car? That way you won't have to walk from the bus stop and get cold."

Yes, he had said those very words. He had said them to Liz Block. He had not said them to Summer Smith. If he had, Summer would now be loving her life instead of hating it.

Just another two blocks to her home, Summer told herself. Two blocks she would not have had to walk if Sean Valletti had asked her to drive with him. Another five minutes of spitting out snowflakes under clouds so low you had to duck to get under them.

There was no sun. There never had been a sun. It was made up by science teachers. And there was no true love, not in the real world. True love existed only on *The Young and the Restless*. In the real world it didn't matter how young or how restless you were: no true love. Maybe she should have told Sean about the dream she'd had. Then he'd know she existed. He'd think she was bizarre and possibly dangerous, but he'd know she existed.

Summer had told most of it to Jennifer Crosby,

her best friend, who was not known for her subtlety. Jennifer had told her she should march right up to Sean and say something like, "You're the man of my dreams. Literally." Right. Jennifer had also suggested that Summer get Sean's attention by "accidentally" bumping into him. Summer had actually tried that. The bruise had healed after a few days.

Summer smiled ruefully at the memory. Okay, so maybe it wasn't a genuine tragedy that Sean Valletti didn't know she existed. A genuine tragedy would be if he *did* know and was deliberately avoiding her.

She was carefully duckwalking up the icy driveway of her house when the wind caught her. She wobbled. She fought for balance. She lost. And Summer's already bad day suddenly got worse.

Ten minutes later she finally opened her front door. And now she really hated her life.

"Is that you, sweetheart?" Her mother's voice.

Summer closed the door behind her, shuddering with relief. She dropped the wet wad of notebook paper on the carpet. Her biology notes, all in loopy blue handwriting, were blotching and running together.

Her mother stepped out of the living room, carrying her reading glasses in one hand and a book in the other. "It *is* you," she said. "How was your day?"

"Oh . . . fine," Summer said. "Except for the part where I fell on my face, scraped my knee, banged my head against the bumper of the car, and

had to chase my biology notes across the yard."
Summer dug a handful of slush out of her collar.

"Your aunt Mallory called," her mother said.

"Uh-huh."

"She wants to know if you'd like to spend the summer down in Florida on Crab Claw Key. You know, she has that big house there now, practically a mansion, so there's plenty of room. And it's right on the water."

Summer stood very still. The wad of slush was melting in her hand. "You mean . . . You mean, she's asking if I want to spend the summer on the beach, in the sun, swimming and . . . and being warm and lying out in the sun and getting tan . . . and going to beach parties and getting windsurfing lessons from sensitive guys with excellent bodies? She wants to know if I'd like that?"

"Well, would you?" her mother asked.

2

Florida. June.
Prophecies of Love and Guy Number One.

There it was! Summer literally bounced in her seat as she looked out the window of the plane. The clouds had broken up, and the plane had emerged into clear sunlight so bright that Summer scrunched up her eyes as she looked down below at a scene so perfect, so intensely beautiful it made her want to cry.

She noticed the guy in the seat across the aisle looking at her and grinning—the guy who looked exactly like Stone on *General Hospital*. She'd heard him tell someone his name was Seth.

Summer blushed and quickly turned sideways in her seat to press her nose against the plastic window, avoiding making eye contact with Stone/Seth.

No more bouncing, she ordered herself. Cool, sophisticated people do not bounce. And from the very first moment in Florida she was going to be the new, improved, much cooler Summer Smith. The sweet, nice, average, boring Summer Smith whose big whoop in life was hanging out at the mall with the same guys who'd known her all her life was going to be left behind.

Below her was a line of islands, green irregular shapes like mismatched jewels strung together by the wavy line of a single highway. Tiny green islands fringed by white surf. Larger islands with houses in neat rows and the white cigar shapes of boats clustered around the shore.

And in every direction the ocean, the Gulf of Mexico, blue where it was deep; green, even turquoise where it was less deep. Here and there the sun reflected off the surface, making a mirror of the ocean.

The plane sank lower. The water was so clear, Summer could see the shadows of boats on the sea bottom. So clear that in places it was as if boats were floating in air, suspended over ripply sand. Scattered on the water were bright splashes of color—crimson, purple, and buttery gold in the sails of windsurfers. And there were long white trails drawn by Jet Skis and motorboats across the blue.

They were over Crab Claw Key, and Summer laughed.

"See something funny?" the woman in the seat beside her asked.

"It's shaped just like a crab's claw," Summer said.

"What is?"

"Um, you know, Crab Claw Key. It's shaped

like a . . . like a crab's claw." She formed her hand into a crab shape and opened and closed the pincers a few times.

"I think maybe that's how it got the name," the woman said.

Very good, Summer told herself. Already you're on your way to impressing the local people with your brilliance. She slid her crab hand down to her side. She was regretting the decision to wear jeans and a purple University of Minnesota sweatshirt. First of all, she was going to be too hot, judging from the blazing sun. Second, it was like wearing a sign that said "Hi, I'm a tourist from the Midwest. Feel free to mock me."

"You here for the summer, huh?" the woman asked. "Maybe you have a job here, or family?"

"An aunt," Summer said. "And a cousin. But I don't have a job, at least not yet, although I definitely have to get one. Mostly I'm just here to lie on the beach and swim and stuff."

The woman nodded seriously. She was an old woman with a face that had the stretched face-lift look, as though each eye was a little too far around the side of her head. "Here to meet boys, too, right? Find romance?"

Summer glanced at Stone/Seth, hoping he had not overheard that particular part of the conversation. "Maybe," Summer admitted in a low voice. "I mean, it would be okay if I did, but that's not why I'm here."

The woman reached inside a voluminous shoulder

7

bag and pulled out an oblong box. "Would you like me to read your cards? No charge, so don't worry."

"Excuse me?"

"Tarot, honey. Tarot cards. That's what I do; I have a little studio just off the main wharf. Normally I'd have to charge you twenty-five dollars." She began laying brightly illustrated cards on the tray. "We'll have to make this quick; we're getting ready to land."

"I guess you know that because you're a fortune-teller, right? About landing soon, I mean."

The woman did not acknowledge the joke. She was laying out the cards.

"Ahh," the woman said.

"Ahh?"

"Hmmm."

"What?" Summer didn't believe in things like tarot cards, but this was hard to ignore.

"You will definitely meet some young men this summer," the woman said.

"Well, I always *meet* guys; I mean, there are guys at school. Half the people there are guys, so—"

"You will meet three young men, each very different, each very important in your life."

Summer glanced at Stone/Seth. Please, let him not be able to hear this. "Well, thanks, ma'am," Summer said brightly.

"Three young men," the woman repeated. "Maybe some more, too, but at least these three."

The pilot announced that they were beginning their approach. The woman sighed and began gathering up her cards.

Summer fidgeted for several seconds. She really didn't believe in superstitious things like tarot cards. But what would it hurt to find out what the woman knew? Or thought she knew. Or, at least, pretended to know.

"Three guys, huh?"

"Three." A knowing, almost smug nod. "Each very different. One will *seem* to be a mystery. One will *seem* to represent danger. One will *seem* to be the right one."

Crab Claw Key rushed up toward them suddenly, each house visible, cars and boats, and then, people lying out on the beach, tiny brown stick figures seeming to stare up at the plane. The shadow of the plane raced across them.

"Seem?" Summer said.

"The future is always shifting," the woman said. "Is your seat belt fastened?"

The wheels touched down. The plane taxied toward the little terminal, and Summer began to feel nervous. "Just act cool," Summer told herself. "Just don't act like some dweeb from Bloomington."

"What?" the lady asked.

"Nothing," Summer said, not convincingly.

"You watch out for the bad one."

"The bad—"

"One will represent mystery. One will be the

9

right one. But that third boy—you'd better watch out for him."

As soon as the plane had come to a stop, Summer pried her carry-on bag from the overhead compartment and shuffled toward the door with the rest of the passengers. The flight attendants were smiling and chattering, "g'bye, havaniceday, bubbye, g'bye" like happy robots, but Summer barely heard them. She was still turning the woman's words over in her head.

She reached the door to the plane, and blazing heat jumped on her like a wild animal. It glued her University of Minnesota sweatshirt to her skin.

Hot. Very, very hot. Hot like crawling inside an oven.

A breeze like a blowtorch caught Summer's long blond hair and lifted it from the back of her neck. She pried open one eye and saw a world of blazing light. Somehow the plane had flown from the earth straight into the sun.

Stone/Seth squeezed past her on the stairs, jostling her with his bag. "Sorry," he said.

"No, it's my fault. I was just looking around," Summer said. "I should have kept moving."

"First time here?" he asked. His eyes were behind very dark shades. His smile was very nice. His smile was very, *very* nice.

"Uh-huh. Yes."

They had reached the bottom of the stairs.

Stone/Seth moved away, walking quickly across the tarmac. Then he turned, walking backward. "Hey, Minnesota, my name is Seth. I'm from Wisconsin. How long you staying and what's your name?"

"Summer!" she yelled.

"Great," he said. "I'm here for the summer too." He waved and turned away.

3

Passion! Hatred! Betrayal!
And All in Just Ten Minutes.

Summer braced herself as she went in through the terminal doors, ready for the inevitable hug, the affectionate assault of "hello-how-are-you-how's-your-dad-and-mom" questions.

But they didn't come. All around her, people squealed and hugged and slapped each other's backs. But no one was waiting for her.

Summer took a hopeful look around and shifted her bag from one shoulder to the other. The crowd broke up and wandered away. Summer began looking more closely at some of the people sitting nearby. She hadn't seen her cousin Diana or her aunt Mallory in years. Not since Christmas four years ago when Diana had been thirteen and Summer had been twelve. Maybe they had changed, maybe they looked different. A lot different.

But no. They weren't there. Maybe they'd forgotten her. Did she even have her aunt's phone number? Sure. Somewhere. Probably. But wait, was she even here on the right day? Was this the right place?

"Don't be a wiener, Summer," she ordered herself. Her aunt and cousin were just a little late. She should just go ahead and pick up her luggage. They'd get here eventually.

As she walked to the baggage claim area, she noticed an obvious fact: virtually everyone was more tan than her. More tan with less clothing. Hers was the only pair of jeans. Hers were the only pants, period, aside from a pair on a security guard.

And the pair Seth wore. He was just a little way ahead, wearing well-worn Levi's that were splotched here and there with white paint.

Summer felt odd, as if she were following him, although obviously they were just two people going in the same direction. And yet, if he suddenly turned around, he'd probably think she *was* following him. Which would be kind of embarrassing.

She came to three stainless steel carousels in a row. One was turning, and from time to time a piece of luggage would slide down the chute. Seth stood there waiting. Summer took a place a few feet away and looked nonchalant. He glanced at her with equal nonchalance.

Summer checked her watch and scanned the room. She put on a perplexed expression, doing a mime of a person waiting for someone who was late. She checked her watch again and frowned.

"You get stood up?"

Seth was suddenly directly beside her. "What? Oh, yes, I guess so. I mean, someone was supposed to pick me up. They aren't here, though." She smiled and then, idiotically, checked her watch again.

"Keep checking," he advised. "You never know when another minute will zip by. By the way, you never told me your name."

"Yes, I did. It's Summer. Summer Smith."

"Oh. Right. Excellent name," he said seriously, as though he'd really thought it over. "Nice to meet you."

He stuck out his hand. Summer took it. They shook hands solemnly. He had rough, strong hands, though he held hers gently. "Wisconsin, huh?" Summer asked.

"Eau Claire," he said. "I'm a senior. I mean, I will be."

"Me too."

"I hope my aunt gets here," Summer added, after trying for several minutes to think of something much cooler to say.

"I'm going to call my grandfather to come pick me up as soon as I grab my bag," Seth said. "If your aunt doesn't show, maybe we can give you a ride." He took off his sunglasses and stuck them in his pocket.

Summer stole a quick sideways glance. Brown? He looked directly at her. She smiled, swallowed hard, and once again looked hard at her watch.

Yes, definitely brown. Warm, smiling brown eyes and a great smile and rough hands.

Seth leaned forward and snatched up a big canvas duffel bag. "That's mine," he said. "You need a hand with yours?"

"No, I can handle them," Summer said.

"Cool. Well, I'll go call my grandfather."

"Okay. Bye."

By the time Summer had retrieved her bags, Seth was over at a bank of phones. She left her mountain of luggage where it was, hoping no one would steal any of it, and went to the phones. She found her aunt's number in her purse, dug a quarter out of her pocket, and dialed.

Three phones away, Seth hung up his receiver and rolled his eyes. His warm, deep brown eyes.

The phone rang in Summer's ear. Four rings. Then an answering machine. "This is Summer. I'm at the airport," she said after the beep. "Is anyone there? Um, okay. I guess you're probably on the way here. I hope. So I'll wait. Bye."

When she looked up again, Seth was gone. Then she spotted him across the hallway standing by an automatic photo booth. He seemed to be trying to feed a dollar bill into a slot. The bill kept getting rejected. It wouldn't hurt to go over, very casually, and just say hi again.

"Hi again," Summer said. "I guess my aunt is on the way to pick me up. No one answered."

"My grandfather isn't home either," Seth said. "It's not his fault, though—I caught an earlier flight.

Why won't this thing take my money? It took the first dollar. Now it won't take the second one."

"You're getting a picture taken?"

He tried again to shove the bill in the slot. "Trying to. I need to get a passport while I'm down here. I'm hoping to go to the Caymans, do some scuba diving down there." He tried the dollar again.

"Here, try a new bill. Sometimes that works," Summer said. She dug a bill out of her bag and slid it easily into the slot.

"Thanks. I should have taken care of this back home but, you know, distractions . . ." He sat on the little round stool and pulled the curtain closed.

Summer saw the light flash once, twice.

"Hey, I have four more shots," Seth said. "You want them?"

"I guess so," Summer said. "I can use them for before and after pictures."

Seth slid open the curtain. Summer had been leaning against the booth, and now they were suddenly very near to each other.

"Before and after what?" Seth asked.

"Tan," Summer explained. "You know, so I can say, look how white I was when I first got there and how tan I got. I'm so pale now and . . ."

For some reason, Seth was staring at her and not saying anything. He looked perplexed, or maybe a little sick. Summer began to feel uncomfortable herself. "You look . . . uh, not pale," Seth said. "I mean, you have really pretty skin."

16

Summer touched her face. A blush was creeping slowly up her throat. "My face is darker than the rest of me," she said. "I mean, you should see the other parts, total whiteness."

The blush grew rapidly worse. *You should see the other parts!* What? *What?* "What I meant was—"

"Go ahead," he said quickly. "Take those other pictures—"

"I just meant my legs are like—"

"Here, just sit and then you make sure your face is—"

"I mean, they're—I didn't mean—"

He moved aside, and she tried to squeeze past him into the booth. They did a stammering little dance, him moving one way, her the other.

He took her shoulders, intending to trade places with her. She looked up at him, intending to make some joke about how uncoordinated they were.

Both of them froze. Seth's eyes seemed to glaze over. He bent down. His face was so close to hers that when she turned her head, his mouth pressed sweetly against her cheek.

They separated in shock. Then, before she knew what was happening, Summer closed her eyes and his mouth met hers in an infinitely sweet, indescribably perfect kiss.

They separated in even greater shock. Summer was too dazed to know what she felt.

"I'm sorry," Seth said quickly. "I didn't mean to—"

Now Summer was beginning to feel something.

Two somethings: ridiculous and embarrassed on the one hand, and very warm and idiotically happy on the other.

Seth turned away abruptly. "I'm really sorry," he repeated. "Really. I mean, I don't . . . I'm not like some jerk who would do this."

"It's okay," Summer said. It was more than okay, but the way Seth was acting was starting to make her feel more embarrassed.

"I gotta go," Seth said. "Call my grandfather. Anyway, bye."

And to Summer's utter amazement, he took off at a fast walk across the terminal.

Diana Olan sat slumped in the passenger seat of her mother's car. She turned the volume dial on the CD player up high enough to allow Green Day's lyrics to be heard by people halfway across the island. Through the dark-tinted windshield she saw the sign for the airport and sighed. She turned the volume knob up a little further still.

Diana's mother reached across and punched the power button with her long, painted fingernail. The music stopped instantly.

"She's going to get picked up by some pervert in that airport," Mallory Olan said.

"I guess that would be bad, right?" Diana reached for the CD player.

"Maybe we'll get lucky and the flight will be late," Mallory said.

"Maybe we'll get really lucky and it will crash."

Diana turned the music back on but cranked the volume only halfway up.

They turned onto the approach road. A plane roared low over their heads.

"Maybe that's her plane," Mallory said. "We'd still get there before she could get off. I don't want her wondering if she's been abandoned, poor kid. I'll bet that's her plane."

"Oh, goody," Diana said. "Should I start jumping for joy now, or should I wait till I actually see little miss sweetness and light?"

"Diana, do we have to do this? You might try being civilized. Summer *is* your cousin, after all, and you're practically the same age."

"Then I guess everything will be perfect," Diana said. "We'll instantly become best friends. We'll bake cookies together and giggle. And slowly but surely I'll turn into Summer and be just like her. That *is* the plan, isn't it?"

Mallory gave her a sour look. Then, with an effort, she forced a pleasant smile. "I kind of like this band. What's their name?"

Diana instantly turned off the music.

Mallory parked the Mercedes in the lane where it said No Parking and checked her face in the mirror. "She'll think I look old."

"Can we just get this over with?" Diana suggested.

Mallory caught the eye of a skycap and pointed at two bags in the backseat. She checked her watch. "At least *I* won't be late," she muttered.

Diana followed her mother into the terminal. As

usual Mallory moved at top speed, like a human express train, swaggering along with the confidence of a person who expects everyone else to clear a path.

"There she is!" Mallory pointed. "Come on, hurry up, Diana. The poor thing's standing there looking like a waif."

Diana slowed down, taking the opportunity to straighten her sarong skirt, which had gotten twisted around while she'd fidgeted in the car. She wore a faded tank top that rode up, revealing a tan, flat stomach. Her feet were bare. Her long dark hair was pulled back in a French braid, accentuating large, arresting gray eyes.

Diana saw Summer weaving her way through the passing crowd: a pretty blond girl with skin from a Noxema ad, carrying electric blue nylon zipper bags and wearing something bulky and purple. Summer was smiling like Miss America and looking depressingly wholesome.

Oh, it was going to be a long, long summer. Unless Diana could get rid of her cousin.

There was no question in Diana's mind why Mallory—Diana had long ago stopped calling her "mother"—had invited Summer down for a visit. Summer was supposed to "normalize" Diana. Mallory had decided that Diana was getting depressed, not doing as well as she should in school, and becoming more private. And the solution? Fly in the happy squad. Bring on cousin Summer.

Then something else caught Diana's eye. Seth Warner, standing by a bank of phones.

Seth glanced around blankly, then did a perfect double take as his gaze met Diana's. She smiled wryly. He looked uncomfortable but gave a little wave before turning away to hide the fact that he was blushing.

Seth Warner. Well, not exactly a big surprise, given the strange phone call Diana had received that morning. His hair was a little shorter, and he'd grown a little more serious looking since the previous summer. Still, she'd recognize that face anywhere—even though it wasn't exactly his face that stuck in her mind.

Summer was still rattled from the encounter in the photo booth, still trying to get her heart to slow down enough to let her catch her breath, when she spotted two familiar faces.

"Is that them?" Summer muttered under her breath. It looked like it might be them, but the airport terminal was full of people. She didn't want to go running up to them and find out she was hugging the wrong people.

But it did look like them, and they were smiling at her. Or at least Aunt Mallory was. Diana was just looking casual and glancing off toward the baggage carousel. Casual in a totally beautiful *Glamour* magazine kind of way. She wasn't even wearing shoes. In an airport. Way cool.

"Summer!" the woman yelled, holding out her arms in a big gimme-a-hug pose.

"Aunt Mallory!" Summer dropped her bag and ran up to her. Aunt Mallory had bigger hair than Summer remembered. Big, stiff hair. Maybe it was because Mallory was famous now, a best-selling romance novelist. Over her aunt's shoulder she caught Diana's eye. Diana made the smallest smile possible and let it linger for about one second.

"I'm so sorry we're late," Aunt Mallory said, holding Summer out at arm's length, inspecting her. "I hope you weren't bored or worried."

Bored? No, definitely not bored. It had been one of the more intense fifteen-minute periods in Summer's life. She felt like a person who'd survived a small earthquake and was still shaky. "No, I wasn't worried. I knew you'd be here."

"Good girl. And how was the flight?"

"It was fine, I guess. I mean, it's not like I've been on lots of planes."

Mallory rolled her eyes very dramatically. "Unfortunately, I *have* been on lots of flights. I feel like I scarcely touch the ground anymore. In fact, I'm just on my way to another one now."

Summer took a moment to digest this. "Did you say you're on your way *now?*"

Mallory made a point of looking at her watch. "Yes, and look at the time. They'll be announcing my flight any minute now. I'm on a book tour. Albany, Syracuse, Cincinnati, and . . . and one of those other places in the Midwest I can never keep straight."

"You're leaving?" Summer asked, still not quite sure she'd understood.

"In ten minutes," her aunt confirmed. "But don't worry; Diana will take care of you and I'll be back in a week. You and Diana are going to be good friends."

Summer glanced hopefully at Diana. Diana didn't look like she was planning on being anyone's friend.

Summer was alone with Diana. Diana was politely carrying the smallest of Summer's several pieces, the video camera she'd brought along, while Summer was loaded down with the rest.

"That's the car," Diana said, pointing at the cream-colored Mercedes convertible.

"*Your* car?"

"While Mallory's away, it is," Diana said.

Summer piled her bags into the backseat. "I hope I didn't bring too much stuff."

"Hey, wait up!" someone yelled.

Seth!

Summer smiled, then decided she'd better not be too obvious and stopped smiling, then changed her mind again.

It didn't matter. Seth had pushed past her as if he'd never met her before. He dropped his bags in front of Diana.

"Well, if it isn't Seth Warner. Back for another summer?"

Seth put on a tight smile. "Diana. Hi. Yeah, I'm back, and look, I, uh, caught an earlier flight, so my grandfather can't come pick me up . . ."

"You need a ride?"

"A cab would cost me ten bucks," Seth explained.

"Pile in," Diana said. "You'll have to squeeze up front with us. This is my cousin, Summer."

"We sort of met," he said stiffly. Then he

laughed, a nice, gentle laugh, still tinged with embarrassment. "Did you say 'cousin'? Summer, you can't be related to Diana—you seem so nice."

Nice. Summer gritted her teeth a little at that word. *Nice*. She'd heard that word too many times in her life. It was the kiss of death when it came to romance. Had she done something wrong when he'd kissed her? Was that why he'd run off?

Diana lowered the top of the convertible. "So," she said to Seth, "is Lianne down yet?"

Seth's gaze met Summer's and then fell away, refocusing on his shoes. "No, I guess she's coming down next week."

Diana pulled the car into traffic. "What's it been, four years with the same girlfriend, Seth? What's the deal? You going for the faithfulness award or something?"

Seth glanced at Summer from under ridiculously long lashes. "Actually, um, Diana, I kind of . . . Lianne and I broke up."

"Oh, really?" Diana drew the word out skeptically. "You and Lianne broke up, huh? Who's next to go? Ken and Barbie?"

"It kind of just happened," Seth said. Again he looked meaningfully at Summer, as if he was trying to send her a message.

Summer looked away.

"When did it happen?" Diana asked.

"It's just been a week," Seth said. Looking again at Summer he added, "It's kind of taking me a while to get over it totally. I guess it's strange to think of being with another girl. Do you know what I mean?"

Summer swallowed hard. Was he making an excuse for walking away after he'd kissed her?

Diana laughed. "It must be even stranger for Lianne to get used to," she said, adjusting her rearview mirror.

"Why do you say that?" Seth asked.

"You said you broke up a week ago?" Diana asked.

"Yes."

"It's just that Lianne called me this morning, asked me if I'd seen you down here yet."

Summer could feel tension in Seth's arm as it rested lightly on her shoulders. He seemed to be holding his breath. "She called you?" he said.

"Lianne is under the impression that we are friends," Diana said with a sneer. "Anyway, you know how she is. She wanted to be sure I gave you a message."

"A message?"

"Yeah." Diana cut across two lanes of traffic. "She said to remind you that she'll be down on Tuesday. And, of course, the other thing."

"What other thing?" Seth asked.

Diana sent him a condescending look. "To tell you that she loves you." Diana laughed and shook her head. "Seth, Seth, Seth. It's not like you to tell lies about breaking up with people. What were you planning to do? Have a little fling with some sweet, unsuspecting tourist girl before Lianne showed up?"

4

A Most Excellent and Luxurious Mansion. But Not for Summer.

W hich pincher is your house on?" Summer asked Diana. She was trying to make conversation. Mostly because she was trying not to think about Seth's arm around her shoulders, resting on the seat back, or his leg pressed against hers. The front seat was cramped with the three of them.

Lianne! No wonder Seth had acted so strange when they kissed. *Lianne.* Boy, it was amazing how such warm, gentle brown eyes could lie. No wonder he'd run off like that. Guilty conscience. And then, Diana had caught him in his lie!

Diana stopped adjusting the rearview mirror and looked at Summer with genuine puzzlement. "Pincher? What are you talking about, Summer?"

"Crab Claw Key," Summer explained, shouting slightly as they passed beneath the highway. "You know, the two pinchers."

"You mean old side and new side," Seth said quietly.

You mean old side and new side, Summer repeated with silent sarcasm. Anything like the old girlfriend and the new girl? Toad. Faithless toad. Kissing Summer like that and making her feel . . . and then: *Lianne.*

"The smaller pincher, the one to the west, is *old side* because that's where the town is and there didn't used be much over on the new side," Diana explained, sounding weary. "Now the new side is all built up. My house is on the old side."

"Oh," Summer said. They were passing a small shopping center on their left. Straight ahead the water was coming into view, marked by a small forest of boat masts. "I saw this monster house over on the big pin—I mean, over on new side, right on the tip. I think they had a helicopter there."

Diana's condescending smile evaporated. "Yeah, that's the Merrick estate."

"Merrick?" Summer repeated. The name sounded vaguely familiar.

"As in *Senator* Merrick," Seth interjected. "As in billionaires."

"No way!"

"All the money in the world and still jerks," Diana said.

Summer could hear the anger in Diana's voice.

"You and Adam Merrick still broken up?" Seth asked Diana. "I was sure you'd be back together by now. How many eighteen-year-old billionaires are you going to run into? I thought you guys were even looking to go to the same college this fall."

"No," Diana said shortly. She bit her lip, and Summer saw her shake her head, just slightly, as if trying to clear an image out of her mind. "I don't think that plan is going to work out."

Diana turned her opaque shades toward Seth. "Although I do miss the parties we used to have over on the Merrick estate, Mr. Moon."

Now it was Seth's turn to look even more uncomfortable. Conversation in the car stopped.

They slowed as they entered the tiny town, just a few streets of white clapboard buildings decorated with sun-faded awnings and quaint hand-lettered signs. The main street was lined at irregular intervals with palm trees, looking wonderfully alien to Summer's eyes.

So what if Diana wasn't very friendly and the first guy she'd met turned out to be a jerk? There were still palm trees! Two tall, stunning, deeply tanned young women dressed in nothing but extremely small bikinis were Rollerblading right down the middle of the street. An old man wearing nothing but shorts and far too much white body hair grinned toothlessly at the car as they glided by. Summer waved and the old man waved back. A perfectly normal-looking family, two parents and two kids, all with blazingly white skin and an assortment of bright shorts and Key West T-shirts, walked along aimlessly.

Diana turned down a side street and stopped the

car in front of a small, neat house shaded by a huge blaze of red flowers.

Seth got out, more or less climbing over Summer in the process. He lifted his bags out of the back.

"See you around," Seth said to both girls. Then, to Summer, "I hope . . . I mean . . ." He sighed resignedly. "Anyway, welcome to Florida."

He still had a very nice smile, even if he was a toad.

"Later," Diana said, and took off.

Summer turned to look back. Seth was carrying his bags toward the door of the house. "Why did you call him Mr. Moon?"

Diana grinned, the first real smile Summer had seen from her. "We were all at a big party at the Merrick estate. Seth was down on their pier, looking off at the sunset. Some guys decided he was being antisocial or whatever and decided to pants him."

"What's that?"

"They yanked off his bathing suit and threw it into the water."

"Oh." Summer wasn't sure she wanted to hear the rest of the story, but it was too late now.

"I used to be into photography back then, and I was already getting ready to shoot the sunset—and Seth standing there looking at it—because I thought it would make a cool shot. Anyway, they pants poor Seth, he dives off to get his bathing suit back, and I click at just the perfect moment." Diana caught Summer's eye and gave her a devious look. "It's a really unique shot."

"Yeah, I'm sure." Summer put a hand over her

heart. She tugged open the neck of her sweatshirt. It was definitely hot here. She didn't want to think about him. What had happened between them was just a mistake. She was going to forget about it, and Seth had better forget about it too. She was going to start this vacation over, beginning now.

"I still have the picture around somewhere," Diana said, obviously enjoying Summer's embarrassment. "I call it 'The Sun . . . and the Moon.'"

The town was soon behind them, and they drove faster down a road that ran right along the edge of the bay. The water could be glimpsed only in flashes between the mismatched array of houses: some new pink stucco mansions, some older, gaily painted wood homes, some simple ranch-style houses that would have been at home in the older parts of Bloomington.

Diana pulled the car into a driveway and under the shade of a portico. She turned off the key. Summer smoothed her tangled hair back into place.

"This is it," Diana said, looking the house over critically. "All the tackiness you'd expect from a semirich romance writer."

"It's huge," Summer said. The house was painted yellow and turquoise and white, a complex jumble of arched windows and fantastic turrets and screened balconies.

"Oh yeah, it's definitely huge. Only . . ." Diana darted a quick look at Summer. And then she smiled. Her second smile, although it wasn't exactly pleasant. "Only not as huge as you'd think. Actually, there are only five bedrooms in the whole place. Mallory and I each have one, of course. And there's one we keep for important guests—you know, people Mallory wants to impress. So that only leaves two."

Summer smiled. "Well, I only need one."

"If only it were that easy," Diana said regretfully. "Come on, I'll show you."

Summer climbed out and began lifting her bags from the backseat. The feeling of nervousness was growing stronger. What did Diana mean, *if only it were that easy*? And wasn't Diana even going to help her carry her bags?

"Don't worry about carrying all your bags at once," Diana said breezily as Summer struggled. "You can always come back for the rest later. If you decide to stay."

If I decide to stay? It was almost as if Diana was trying to get rid of her. In fact, it was *exactly* as if Diana was trying to get rid of her.

Diana was quite proud of herself. It had come to her in a flash of inspiration. Of course! It was so simple. If she moved Summer into one of the regular bedrooms, she'd never get rid of her cousin. Face it, it was a great house. Who wouldn't want to stay in a designer-decorated bedroom overlooking the water, with a private bath and a private balcony and a housekeeper to make your bed?

Mallory had already picked out the perfect room for Summer. Way too perfect. No, Diana had a much better idea for where Summer should stay.

And with Mallory out of town, well, why not? With any luck at all, Summer would be on the next plane out of town.

Diana conducted Summer through the house at a virtual run. Here's the kitchen, oh, yes, it is huge. Here's the family room. Oh, yes, it's huge, too. Here's the game room, no, I don't play pool, the pool table's only there because you need a pool table to make it a game room. Here's my room, and here's Mallory's room . . .

"Why do you call your mother Mallory?" Summer asked.

"Because that's her name. She calls me Diana because that's *my* name. That's the way it works." Diana winced. Now she was getting *too* mean. That wasn't right. It wasn't Summer's fault she wasn't wanted here. Besides, if Diana was too cruel, Summer might get upset and start crying or something, and then what?

But Summer didn't burst into tears.

"I call my mother Mom," Summer said matter-of-factly. "So, where am I staying?"

"You know I told you there were two bedrooms left? Well, see, the problem is that one is being redecorated, so it's a mess." Technically true, Diana told herself. Her mother *was* waiting on a new dresser for that room. "And the problem with the other room is . . ." Diana paused. Was Summer going to buy this at all? Only one way to find out. "The problem with the other room is that Mallory . . . Mom . . . has to have it available for when she gets hysterical."

Summer looked wary but not completely disbelieving. "Hysterical?"

Diana nodded sagely. "Hysterical. It happens sometimes when Mallory . . . Mom . . . starts remembering Dad—you know, the divorce and all, and the good times they had and so on. Then she gets hysterical, see, because, well, her bedroom used to be *their* bedroom, and then it's like all these memories come back and she . . . she, uh, has to sleep in the other bedroom," Diana finished lamely. "That's why there's like no room. In the house."

Right, Summer thought. Does she think I'm a complete idiot? Diana was definitely *not* making her feel welcome. Fine. So Diana hated her for some reason. Fine. So Diana wanted to get rid of her. That was fine too. Only it wasn't going to be that easy.

"So where am I supposed to stay?" Summer asked. "Am I supposed to sleep on the couch?"

"No, that wouldn't work. But there *is* a place for you." Diana showed her brief, fake smile. "There's a definite place for you. Follow me."

Summer followed Diana downstairs, down one of the twin, curving staircases that looked like something out of a movie, through the gigantic living room and out onto the porch, where the heat was waiting to pounce on her again.

They walked down across a sloping, green lawn toward the water, toward the spot where a cabin cruiser was tied up to the pier. They turned left, aiming at a stand of trees. The shade of the trees was welcome. And then Summer saw it.

It was a bungalow, squat and homely, white paint chipped and faded, looking forlorn and abandoned. It would have looked like any way-below-average house in any way-below-average neighborhood except that it was raised on wooden stilts and stood directly over the water. A shaded stairway seemed to run from the interior of the house straight down to a small platform on the water. Two Jet Skis were tied up there, knocking together haphazardly on the gentle swell.

A rickety-looking wooden walkway ran a hundred feet from the grassy, shaded shore to the house. The walkway wrapped around the house, forming a narrow deck lined with a not-exactly-reassuring railing. A pelican sat on one corner of the railing, its huge beak nestled in its brown feathers. As Summer watched, the pelican added to the crusty pile of droppings.

"It has a bedroom, a kitchen, and a bathroom," Diana announced proudly.

"And a pelican who thinks the whole thing is a bathroom," Summer said.

"You'd have a lot of privacy here," Diana said, trying unsuccessfully to keep from gloating. "Sure, there's a little mildew, some pelican droppings, and you know, the furniture isn't exactly the very best . . ."

"This is where Aunt Mallory wants me to stay?" Summer asked dubiously.

"Oh, she's not much for details of who stays

where," Diana said, waving a hand breezily. "You'll be thrilled to know that this is a historical house; that's why Mallory doesn't tear it down. It was used by rum smugglers back during Prohibition in the 1920s. And we were renting it out until a couple of years ago."

"Uh-huh," Summer said. So this was Diana's plan to get her to leave. She was going to stick her here in mildew manor. Diana probably thought she'd just start boohooing and run home to her mother. Well, maybe she should, if no one wanted her here.

Only, Summer didn't like to get pushed around. She was here to have an excellent summer vacation, even if it meant living with the pooping pelican.

"Do I get to use the Jet Skis?" Summer asked tersely.

Diana looked surprised. "Um, sure. I mean, if you're staying, I guess . . ." Her voice drifted away.

"Of course I'm staying," Summer said. "This place looks beautiful and perfect, and you and I are going to become best friends, just like Aunt Mallory said." Take that, witch, Summer added silently.

Diana swallowed. For the first time she looked unsure of herself. "We are?"

5

*L*ive, from fabulous Crab Claw Key, it's . . . Summer Smith!

Okay, okay. Hello, Jennifer. I said I would keep this video diary for you, and here's the first one. I barely know how to run this stupid video camera, so if the picture's all jerky don't blame me.

What you are looking at right now is my incredibly luxurious bedroom. You will notice the way the bed sort of sags and droops in the middle—very fashionable. And now you can see the kitchen. You say it looks like it's practically in the bedroom? Funny you should mention that; it sort of *is*. That's my stove. I think someone *may* have cleaned it once, about ten years ago. Refrigerator. Hang on, let me open it. See? Someone stocked it with exactly three cans of Pepsi and a half-eaten bag of Nacho Doritos.

Here's the bathroom. Cool tub, huh? I mean, it's got some rust stains, but it's huge, and see, it's one of those old-timey claw-foot tubs.

But the tub isn't the most excellent part of this place. No, the really neat thing is where the house is. See this square door in the floor? Hang on, let me pull it open. Urrgh. That's heavy, but can you see? Water. Right downstairs, that's actual seawater because this place is right over the water.

Is that great or what?

Okay, outside. Follow me. Like you have any choice. The front door . . . and look! This little deck goes all the way around the house. And see? There's the walkway. See? It's like fifty feet or whatever to the shore.

Okay, now, there's the main house. You have to kind of look *through* those trees to see all of it. I know what you're thinking, Jen. You're thinking whoa, that looks like a mansion and Summer's living in a shack. Okay, that may be true. However, this shack is all mine. Besides, there are Jet Skis and I'm going to learn how to—oh, jeez, oh, oh, yuck. Gross. I brushed against some pelican stuff on the railing. Great. This pelican kind of lives here. There. There he is, diving for food. Isn't that excellent the way he does that?

Okay, back inside. Here, I'm going to put this down on the table and then I'll sit right in front of it.

Okay. Now can you see me? Hi. As you can see,

it's not like I have a tan yet. I just got here like an hour ago.

So far everything's fine. Except that my cousin—Diana, the one who lives here?—I think she hates me. I think it was her big idea to stick me out here in the stilt house because her mom, who is my aunt, is out of town for a week. So I'm stuck with cousin Diana, who doesn't want to be stuck with me, I guess.

Okay, I'm not getting bummed. Just because Diana thinks I'm like some hopeless case, that's just what *she* thinks.

Although she *is* totally cool; I mean, she's one of those girls you and I can't stand, you know? She looks like that model they always have in *Sassy*, you know the one I mean?

Anyway. I guess it will be better when my aunt Mallory gets back. I hope so, since Mom and Dad are off on vacation themselves and my plane ticket is for three months from now. So I'm stuck, no matter how much Diana doesn't like it. I'm stuck here in mildew world.

I'm not crying.

Okay, I am crying, but just a little. It's been a stressful day. There was this one guy I met. Okay, more than met, but it's a whole long story, so let me just give you the short version: he's a using little creep.

You see, there was this . . . this thing that happened with him. In the airport. I'll tell you later when I'm done feeling weirded out by it.

Oh, and there are supposed to be two other guys too, if you believe in that kind of stuff. But okay, later on all that. Anyway, I'm going to turn this thing off. I have to unpack and try to clean this dump up a little, and it's starting to get dark out. Let's hope this summer gets better fast.

6

First Night.
Strange Dreams and Stranger Realities.

Summer lay in her bed. It definitely sagged in the middle.

Earlier she'd gone up to the main house, called her mother to let her know she'd made it to Florida alive, and gotten some sheets and a blanket from Diana, feeling like Oliver Twist begging for more gruel. Diana had seemed friendly in about the same way that a cat seems friendly to a mouse.

Maybe I should just give up and go home, Summer thought miserably. "Too bad that's impossible," she muttered into the darkness.

It was a little creepy inside the stilt house with the lights out. A silvery shaft of moonlight had appeared in her window, illuminating her desk and the video camera resting there. It made her think of her best friend, Jennifer, and that made her think of home. Home, with her familiar bedroom, and all her posters and photos on the wall, with her CDs neatly in their rack.

Summer kicked off the single blanket and pulled the sheet over her. It was hot in the house, even with all the windows open. Even the boxers and baby-tee she wore to bed felt like too much.

"Hot and depressed and lonely," she told the stifling air. "So far it's a great vacation." If she were home, she'd go get some ice cream from the freezer.

From the windows she heard the sound of the water lapping gently at the pilings that supported the house. When the Jet Skis rocked there was a hollow sound, like coconuts being knocked together softly. And the house itself creaked and groaned, but in an almost musical way.

It was sometime later that the video camera seemed to turn on and begin projecting a flickering image on the wall, like an old-fashioned home movie. Summer saw a backyard scene, the yard of her house in Bloomington. The swing set her parents had bought for her third birthday. The little play pool, filled with plastic toys. Her Oscar the Grouch! She hadn't seen Oscar in years. Whatever had happened to good old Oscar?

Summer rose from her bed and moved toward the images. Her mother was in the picture now, gazing at her with that familiar look of concern. The look that said *Sometimes, Summer, I swear you worry me.*

"Come on out of there," her mother said, holding out her hand. Summer looked down and realized she was covered in mud. What a mess. The pelican, who was now swimming in her pool, was trying to look innocent, but obviously he was responsible.

Suddenly Summer was in her room back home, looking down at her bed, only the bed kept shrinking till it was the size of a doll bed. It made Summer angry, though she wasn't sure why. Something caught her eye. Three cards lay in a row on the covers. Two were facedown. One was turned up, and when Summer looked closer she saw it was a photograph—a photograph of a red sun and a pale, white moon. The moon made her feel very uncomfortable.

Then, all at once, Summer was back in the stilt house, hearing some new noise to add to the creaks and groans and lapping water. The flickering images of home faded out and disappeared.

Her eyes opened. A creaking sound, very clear, *very* clear and real and not a part of the dream. A creaking sound and now a tuneless, almost random humming.

Summer lay perfectly still. The sound had come from very close. But she was turned away from it and not willing to roll over to see what it might be.

It was the hatch in the floor! That's what it had to be. The hatch that led down to the water, down to where the Jet Skis were. Down to where some monster, some ax murderer, some creature that had been lying, waiting for her to fall asleep so he could creep up the stairs and come in through the hatchway and kill her, hacking her up with a machete.

Summer rolled ever so slightly. Now the room

didn't seem so hot. No, it had definitely gotten chillier. She wished she had her blanket back. She could pull it over her head and hope the monster—ax-murderer went away.

A light!

Summer slitted her eyes and stared, barely able to breathe. A blue–white light emanated from the kitchen.

The humming stopped and was replaced by a mixture of whistling and humming. The tune became recognizable. It sounded like "Head Like a Hole."

No way. Ax murderers didn't listen to Nine Inch Nails. On the other hand, it *was* pretty good ax murderer music.

The light in the kitchen disappeared. From the darkness came the distinctive sound of a pop–top. The whistling stopped. A satisfied sigh.

A lighter flickered, and then a candle, a brilliant yellow pinpoint of light in the dark, illuminating a startling sight.

"Aaargh!" the figure yelled.

"Aaargh!" Summer jumped back as if she'd been electrocuted, snatching her sheet around her like a shield.

"Wh–what are you—"

"Who—what are you—get out of here!"

"Chill out, don't shoot or anything!"

"Don't kill me, I'm from Minnesota!"

A silence, during which Summer listened to the panic-driven jackhammer beat of her heart. Her teeth rattled.

43

"Did you just say 'Don't kill me, I'm from Minnesota'?"

"Uh–uh–uh–uh, yes," Summer chattered.

"What's Minnesota got to do with anything?"

"Uh, nothing, I guess."

"Who *are* you?" he asked, coming warily closer.

Now Summer could see that he wasn't a monster. He could still be an ax murderer, but not a monster. He had long, wet, shoulder-length blond hair and wore only a madras bathing suit that clung to him damply.

"I'm Summer. Sum–sumsum–sum Summer Smith."

"Oh."

"Who are you?" Summer managed to ask. Her voice sounded strained with the tightness in her throat and the still-chattering teeth.

"I'm Diver."

"Diver?"

"Yeah." He sounded defiant. "Like *Summer* is some kind of normal name?"

"What are you doing here?" Summer demanded.

"What am *I* doing here?" Diver asked, mildly outraged. He took a sip of his Pepsi and sat the candle down on her desk, balancing it carefully. "What are *you* doing here?"

"Living here," Summer said. "And people know I'm here, so don't try anything."

"*I* live here," Diver said. "At least, I mean, I use the bathroom and the kitchen here. I don't sleep here." He pulled out the desk chair. "I usually sleep up on the roof."

"You can't live here; my aunt owns this place."

"Oh. She's that rich lady with really big hair?"

"Yes."

"Well, I don't care who owns it," Diver said. "I live here. I've been coming here for . . . for like months."

"Fine, I'm not going to call the cops or anything," Summer said. "Just go away and don't come back. Okay?" She was gaining courage from the fact that Diver hadn't done anything sudden. Yet. And, not that you could tell just by looking, but he didn't *look* dangerous. In fact, by the candle's light he looked . . . beautiful. There was no other word for it. Beautiful.

"Where am I supposed to take a shower and cook breakfast and sleep when it rains?"

Summer shrugged. "I don't know."

"Yeah, I didn't think you'd have an answer for that," Diver said triumphantly.

"You sure can't live with me, and I live here, so that's it," Summer said flatly.

"Go stay in your aunt's house," Diver said. "She must have plenty of room."

"I can't," Summer said. "I can't stay there, I can't go home to Bloomington, I have to stay here. I'm stuck."

"Me too," Diver said. "We're both stuck."

"Excuse me, but whatever you're thinking, forget it," Summer said, crossing her arms over her chest. "I don't, like, go out with guys I meet creeping into my room in the middle of the night."

"I don't go out with girls at all."

"Oh. Are you . . . not that it's any of my business. I mean, I don't have a problem if you're gay or anything like that . . ."

Diver tilted back his head and looked at her with a certain distant intensity. "I no longer involve myself with women. They disturb my *wa*."

"Wa?"

"My *wa*. My inner harmony. Haven't you ever read any eastern philosophy?" Diver smiled placidly, looking quite smug and superior. Then the smugness dropped away. "But I'm not gay," he said. "Not that I would care. I'm just saying I'm not. If I were, then women wouldn't disturb my *wa* the way they do."

"Whatever. Just get out, okay?"

Diver stood up. "It's a beautiful night. I'll sleep outside with Frank."

"Fine. Whatever you say. Just leave."

He turned away and headed for the door. He stopped with his hand on the knob. "Frank isn't a dude, by the way, so forget it if that's what you're thinking." He nodded as if he'd reached some profound decision. "Tomorrow I'll talk to Frank. Then *he* can decide which of us stays and which goes."

Summer rushed over as soon as he was gone and locked the door behind him. Then she ran back and, huffing and grunting, slid the desk over the hatchway.

"There," she muttered. "Now you and your *wa* will have a real hard time getting back in."

7

Raisin Toast, Imaginary Figments, and the Amazing Marquez

Diana took a while looking through the contents of her walk-in closet, searching for the right thing to wear. The right thing turned out to be white shorts and a white bikini top. White reflected sunlight and hence was cooler than other colors.

Also, white looked innocent. And, she decided as she descended the stairs, she needed all the help she could get in looking innocent. She didn't *feel* innocent. She felt like a selfish, rotten human being who had tricked her cousin into spending the night in a mildewy dump. Once in the dark hours of the early morning she'd almost gotten up and gone down to the stilt house to get Summer and bring her back.

But really, she was doing Summer a favor. Summer might think she wanted to be here, but that was only because Summer didn't understand anything.

The set of stairs led directly from just outside

her room to the breakfast room. And there, sitting at the long pine table, was Summer. At least her cousin hadn't been murdered in the night. That was a relief. Diana didn't need any new reasons to hate herself.

Summer looked up from her plate and smiled. Smiled that big, happy-yet-shy smile that made you think you'd never seen anyone whose name so matched her looks.

"Hi," Summer said, chewing. "I hope it's all right. I don't have any food down at my house yet."

"Of course it's all right," Diana said quickly. She tried out her most innocent look. "You have to eat."

"Thanks."

"Did you find everything you want?" Diana asked. "I mean, here in the kitchen."

"Yeah, all I eat is raisin toast for breakfast, mostly."

"Raisin toast?" Diana narrowed her eyes suspiciously. "That's what I have in the morning too."

"No way." Summer laughed a little and looked amused.

"What?" Diana demanded.

"Nothing. It's just, I figured you had something different. Like eggs Benedict or something."

Diana went to the toaster. The bread was still out on the gray marble counter. "Why would I eat eggs Benedict?"

Summer shrugged. "I don't know. That was just the most fancy breakfast thing I could think of. You always hear about movie stars having eggs Benedict and champagne."

"No champagne," Diana said dryly. "Coffee. You drink coffee?"

Summer nodded. "Only, I couldn't figure out how to work your machine."

"I'll do it. It's kind of complicated." Diana dumped whole beans into the grinder, sent them spinning, and then measured the grounds into the coffee machine. "Coffee and raisin toast," she muttered, watching the back of Summer's head.

"Every morning almost. I'll have to buy a toaster and a coffee machine for my house."

A little stab of guilt made Diana wince. "How . . . um, how was . . . did you sleep okay?"

Summer turned around in her chair, but her blue eyes were evasive. "I slept okay, I guess. I was going to ask you, though . . ."

"Ask me what?" Diana almost snapped.

"Just that I was wondering if you knew of anyone who used the stilt house for anything."

Diana shrugged. Her toast popped up. The coffee began to dribble down, sending the aroma through the room. "No one's used it for anything in two years, at least. Not since the last renter moved out."

"Huh."

"Why?"

Summer sighed heavily and again looked evasive. "I don't know. I think I just had this dream that some guy was there. But when I got up, there was this burned candle and one of the Pepsis was gone. I guess I could have been walking in my sleep."

"You walk in your sleep?" Diana wondered.

"No. Never before, anyway. I dream a lot, though, and in my dreams I walk around."

"I try not to dream," Diana said.

Silence fell between them. The coffee machine dripped and then began its final sputtering.

"He was cute, though," Summer said.

"Who? The dream guy?" Diana poured two cups of coffee and carried them with her toast to the table.

"Yeah, he was *way* cute. Beyond cute."

"Then it *must* have been a dream," Diana pronounced. "A figment of your imagination."

"I guess so," Summer agreed. "Do you ever have dreams like that?"

"Me?" The question took Diana by surprise. "No, at least not that I remember."

"Do you have a boyfriend?"

Diana squirmed a little in the chair. "Not right at the moment."

"I've never had one," Summer admitted. "Not a real one."

Diana made a face. "Yeah, right."

"It's true. Why would I make up something like that?"

The confession, made so simply and straightforwardly, took Diana aback. There was nothing wrong with not having a boyfriend—in fact, in Diana's experience it was probably better that way—but Summer was just so out front about it. Most girls would have tried to act cooler about it.

Like, hey, the guys are after me, but they're all too immature.

"I guess you've probably had lots of boyfriends," Summer said.

"One or two," Diana admitted. This was the wrong topic. The absolutely wrong topic. It was as if Summer had some instinct guiding her to the last thing on earth that Diana wanted to talk about.

"There was a guy back home that I really liked, only he didn't know I existed." Summer made a wry, self-deprecating face. "I have much better luck in my dreams."

Diana laughed and then quickly took a sip of her coffee. She'd have to watch herself. For a moment there she'd found herself kind of liking her cousin. "So, what are you going to do today?"

"I'm going to look around and maybe get a job," Summer said. "Would you come with me? I mean, unless you have something planned?"

"Why would you want me to come with you?" What was it with this girl? Why was she so nice? She wasn't an idiot; she *must* know Diana was trying to blow her off.

"I thought it might be fun," Summer said. "Besides, I'm new here, so if I go around with you everyone will think 'oh, okay, she must not be a total nobody if she's with Diana.'"

Diana finished her coffee and stared darkly at the bottom of her cup. Yes, she was definitely going to have to work at disliking her cousin.

★   ★   ★

51

In the end Diana decided not to come with her into town, and Summer was actually relieved. It was a wonderful feeling to be walking along the road, free, on her own, almost undisturbed by traffic, feeling the sun on her shoulders and arms. She turned her face to the sun, already most of the way up the sky though it wasn't yet ten in the morning.

A huge, brilliantly white bird, almost chest tall, stepped on stilt legs out onto the road before her. It tilted its serpentine neck to turn a quizzical eye on Summer.

"Hi," Summer said, standing still so as not to frighten it. But the egret wasn't frightened in the least. It tiptoed gracefully across the road.

"Reminds me of Diana," Summer said. Diana had that same grace, that same elegance.

That same disdain.

Too bad, Summer thought. She'd felt as if she were almost bonding with her cousin over raisin toast and coffee, but then Diana had pulled away again.

Summer shrugged. It was impossible to feel bad when the sun was in the sky and the air was warm. She stuck her arms straight out and tilted back her head, soaking up the light, closing her eyes to see the red suffusing her eyelids.

Something slapped into her left arm.

"Hey, watch where you're swinging those!" someone yelled.

Summer opened her eyes and saw a girl running in place, pumping her arms, sweat staining her spandex top. She had dark curly hair; huge, dark eyes;

and a naturally dark complexion. A tape player hung on her hip, and headphones rested on her head.

"Sorry," Summer said. "I thought I was alone."

"Can't hear you. You like the sun, huh?" the girl shouted, still running in place.

"Yes!" Summer yelled.

"Cool!" The girl ran in circles around Summer. "You're new, right?"

Summer turned slowly to keep facing her. "Yes. I just got here yesterday."

"Huh?"

"Yesterday!" Summer said in a louder voice. "I just got here yesterday."

"When?"

"YESTERDAY."

"Huh?"

"I SAID YESTERDAY!" Summer screamed.

The girl stopped running and broke up laughing. She pulled the earphones from her head. She bent over, hands on her knees, laughing and looking up at Summer with tears in her eyes. "Batteries are dead," the girl managed to gasp, pointing at the tape player.

Summer was annoyed for a moment. But then, it *was* kind of funny. She laughed at the image of herself, screaming at the top of her voice.

The girl stopped laughing and looked at her quizzically. "You laugh, huh? That's a good thing." She pointed a finger at Summer. "I can't stand people who can't laugh at themselves. People that take themselves all serious. I'm Marquez."

"You're what?"

"Marquez. That's my name. Technically it's Maria Esmeralda Marquez, but hey, every Cuban-American female on earth is named Maria, right, and there's no way I'm going to be called Esmeralda, so I go by Marquez." She extended a damp hand.

"I'm Summer Smith," Summer said, shaking her hand.

"I don't think so. *Summer?*"

"I'm afraid it's true."

"Yeah? Well, let me ask you, Summer—you think my thighs are too fat?" Marquez turned around so Summer could check all angles.

"No, not at all," Summer answered honestly.

"All right. In that case, why should I be out here running? I hate exercise. What are you doing?"

Summer shrugged. "I was going to check out the town."

Marquez laughed. "That should kill about five minutes."

"Plus I have to find a job," Summer said.

They set off toward town, walking side by side, with Marquez drying her face on her terry-cloth wristbands. "Job? What kind of job you want? What do you know how to do?"

"Nothing, really," Summer admitted.

"Oh, in that case I know where you can get a job, you poor girl."

"Really?" Summer asked eagerly.

"Yeah, the C 'n' C is looking for more victims, I mean, waitresses. The Crab 'n' Conch. Picture this—

a restaurant run by the Marines. Except they're not actually Marines, because then, you know, they'd have to have *some* decency."

"I don't know how to be a waitress."

"That's okay. They don't want people who know what they're doing. They like to get them young and impressionable; you know, so they can mold you into a perfect robot. I know all this because I work there."

"You make it sound really fun," Summer said dryly.

Marquez grinned. "It's hateful, but with the tips and all it's good money. I'll take you there and introduce you to one of the managers. So, where are you staying?"

"My aunt and my cousin live here."

"Yeah? Who are they? I probably know them. I know everyone. It's a small island."

"My aunt is Mallory Olan, and my cousin's Diana."

Marquez stopped and stared, incredulous. "You're staying with Diana Olan? Wait a minute—you're *related* to Diana Olan?"

"She's my cousin, on my dad's side of the family. You know her?"

"Sure. She's in school, or at least she was, because now she's graduated. You can't be related to Diana," Marquez said. "You seem way too nice and normal."

Summer winced. There it was again—the *N* word. Nice. Nice, meaning average, meaning who cares?

"You're the second person who's said that," Summer said.

"Who was the first?"

"This guy named Seth."

"Mr. Moon! Mr. Moon is back? All right, the summer is starting to pick up," Marquez said. "He's a nice guy."

Summer nodded. Some nice guy. A nice guy who lied about having a girlfriend so he could . . . Summer shuddered a little. Why wasn't she able to just forget that stupid kiss? Why did it still seem to reverberate through her body whenever she thought about it?

"Nice *and* cute," Marquez said appreciatively. "Not my type, though. Besides, he's got this girlfriend he's been going with forever. Was she with him?"

"No. Lianne, right?"

"Yeah, Lianne." Marquez stuck her finger down her throat and made a gagging noise.

"You don't like Lianne?" Summer asked, trying not to sound hopeful.

"She's okay. She's just one of these totally dependent types. You know, hanging all over Seth and not letting him have fun. I wish I had her body, though. She shops petites. Complains because she can't find things in size two."

Summer nodded. Lianne would have to have a great body.

Forget about it, Summer, she told herself firmly. Get over it. Put it behind you. Jeez, it was just a kiss. Big deal. Actually, it was two kisses. That doesn't matter; it was just something that happened. Forget about it.

Marquez interrupted her thoughts. "So, Summer, since you're staying with Diana, tell me this—is it true she sleeps in a coffin at night? Oh, maybe I shouldn't say things like that. I mean, she is your cousin and all."

"I don't really know her that well," Summer admitted.

"Actually, she's not so bad," Marquez said. "Just strange, you know? Stays to herself, especially in the past year. I mean, she was always kind of private, right? But this last year it's like no one is even allowed to talk to her because she's become just way too cool."

"She isn't a really friendly person," Summer agreed cautiously. "But that's okay."

"Yeah, not a *real* friendly person," Marquez said, and laughed. "She used to at least hang out, and she was going out with Adam Merrick. She was going with him, and he goes everywhere so she was being more social. Then, boom. Like maybe last July she suddenly dumps Adam cold. He's totally great looking, also totally rich and nice and not stuck-up, and she dumps him."

Summer digested this information. Whatever Diana was lacking in terms of friendliness, Marquez certainly made up for. The girl talked a mile a minute and had barely paused to breathe.

"So ever since she broke up with Adam, it's been bye-bye Diana. She showed up at school, and that's it. We're all thinking it's like some R. L. Stine book or something, like she's turned into a teen vampire, you know?"

"I've seen her in the sunlight, and she hasn't burst into flames or anything," Summer said.

Marquez laughed appreciatively, an infectious sound that brought answering laughter from Summer. "You are definitely all right, girl. I like you. Come on and I'll do something really mean to you. I'll get you a job at the C 'n' C."

8

Marquez's Rules and Diana's Dolphins

Marquez waited outside the restaurant on the wharf and kicked back, leaning against a rough wood piling, legs stretched out in front of her. She looked down at them critically. They weren't pudgy, exactly, but they weren't as hard and lean and muscular as she'd have liked. And her behind, well, that didn't even bear thinking about.

"Stay off the conch fritters, Marquez," she ordered herself sternly. She wasn't going to get fat like her mother. That was fine for her mother, but Marquez had plans for the future. Finish high school, then college, then law school, then get a job as an associate at some big Washington or New York law firm and make partner. She needed to be in shape. She needed to look good in one of those boring skirt suits that lawyers wore. She needed to be able to go to the health club and play squash or racquetball with the partners.

And in the meantime, it didn't hurt to look good for guys.

The door of the restaurant opened, and the new girl, Summer, came out. She looked a little dazed, blinking like an owl in the sunlight. But she was carrying a menu, an employee manual, and a plastic-wrapped uniform. Big surprise. The C 'n' C was always looking for fresh meat. Mostly because people kept quitting. She would quit herself except that certain people still worked there. Certain people she should just forget about.

Forget it, Marquez, set it aside. He was forgotten. He was history. He was something she had scraped off the bottom of her shoes.

"Hey, you got the job, huh?" she asked.

Summer squinted and located Marquez. "Yeah, I did get it. Only . . ." She looked back over her shoulder at the restaurant door and lowered her voice. "Only, I don't know how to do anything."

Marquez laughed. "Nothing to it. I'll have the head waitress put you with me for the first couple days. I'll show you what to do."

"Thanks," Summer said. "That would be really, really nice of you. Thanks for recommending me for this job."

"Wait till you see what you look like in that uniform, *then* you can thank me, if you still want to," Marquez said. "Not to mention the fact that it's very hard work."

"The manager said it was like a big family."

"Yeah. The Manson family. Or the Menendez

family. Or maybe the Addams family. So, now what?"

"What do you mean?"

"I mean, hey, it's not even noon, what have you got planned for the day?"

Summer shrugged. "I guess I thought I'd just look around."

"Yeah? You got anything on for tonight?"

"I don't think so."

"How about you go to this party with me?"

"What party?"

"Adam Merrick's having a party. He has them all the time, over on his daddy's estate."

Summer felt a rush of excitement, chased immediately by a wave of nervousness and uncertainty. Right. Like *she* should be going to parties at some billionaire's house. "I better not," she said. "I mean, he doesn't even know me or anything. I couldn't just show up."

"Where are you from, Summer?"

"Um, Bloomington, Minnesota. It's the home of the Mall of America, the biggest mall in the world." Stop saying things like that! Summer ordered herself. No one cares about the mall!

"Oh, I see. And people up in Bloomyburg are probably real polite and all, right? But see, this is Crab Claw Key. The rules are all different here. Mostly the rule is that there aren't any rules. You wear what you want. You go where you want. You say what you want. You *be* what you want. Nobody here is going to care if you're white or black or gay or straight or whatever religion you are or where you come from, all that stuff. As long as you're cool and don't hassle people and don't be all judgmental, everyone's equal."

Summer nodded. "Okay. I understand, but still—"

Marquez waved her hand dismissively. "And the only other rule is—when there's a party, *everybody* is invited."

"Okay. I get it. Okay." Summer sucked in a deep breath of hot, wet air. She was going to go for it. What good was summer vacation if you didn't take some chances? "But what should I wear?"

"Here's our old friend, Jerry. Would you like to touch him today? He's very nice, you know." Diana held the child safely in her arms, just letting the little girl's feet dangle in the water of the pool. The water came only a little higher than Diana's waist and was almost as warm as a bath.

Jerry floated patiently alongside, knowing his role, breathing softly through his blowhole.

The child, whose name was Lanessa, pointed wordlessly at the blowhole.

"Yes, that's pretty neat, isn't it?" Diana said. "That's how he breathes."

Jerry rolled partially in the water so he could see the little girl more clearly.

"He's smiling," Lanessa said.

"He sure is," Diana agreed. "Jerry likes to smile. You know why? Because Jerry is a very nice dolphin. He especially likes little girls just like you."

Lanessa nodded solemnly, still uncertain. Then

she stuck out her hand, fingers splayed, not quite able to reach. But Jerry drifted closer, bringing his gray snout into contact, accepting the little girl's clumsy patting.

Lanessa patted the dolphin's head for several seconds, then pulled away again. No smile had formed on her lips, but for a few seconds there had been that light in her eyes, the light Diana had seen many times before, when child met dolphin.

"All done?" Diana asked. "You want to say bye-bye to Jerry?"

Lanessa opened and closed her hand, a silent good-bye.

"We'll come see Jerry again soon if you'd like. Do you think that would be fun?"

Lanessa had no answer. The light was gone for now.

"That's okay, Lanessa, you don't have to answer," Diana said softly. She slowly carried the child back to the side of the pool. Two other volunteers were working farther away with two other abused children like Lanessa, showing them there were still safe places in the world.

The Dolphin Interactive Therapy Institute brought children who had lost the capacity to trust together with dolphins. A silly-sounding idea that worked just the same. There was something in the basic gentleness of the big, powerful animals that seemed to calm fears and lure children out of their shells.

Diana helped the little girl get changed and brought her back to the nursery. "Lanessa and Jerry had a good time today," Diana told Dr. Lane, one of the therapists. "She patted Jerry right on his head, didn't you, Lanessa?"

"Well, Jerry is a very special dolphin," Dr. Lane agreed in the deliberately calm, soothing voice they all used for the children.

Diana gave the little girl a kiss on her forehead and said good-bye.

There was a report to be filled out, a complete report detailing precisely how Lanessa had reacted, what she had said (not much), whether she had become agitated (no), whether she had exhibited any signs of panic (also no). Diana did this on a computer in a small cubicle of an office that was shared by all the volunteers.

Then she wrapped a sarong skirt around her barely damp bathing suit and went out to the parking lot, feeling the strange mixture of elation and weariness followed by slow, spreading melancholy she usually felt on leaving the institute.

The institute was on Cannonball Key, twenty miles up the highway from Crab Claw Key. Diana traveled south, heading home, driving her own car, a blue, year-old Neon. Somehow driving her mother's Mercedes to the institute, where even the professional counselors drove ten-year-old Volvos and minivans, would have seemed too showy.

The sun was still high in the sky, barely weakening in the long summer day. A bank of storm clouds was building up in the east, towering as high as a chain of mountains. Far-off flashes of lightning struck the water again and again.

What was she going to do about Summer? Diana asked herself. Presumably the girl would still be there when Diana got home.

Unacceptable. Diana didn't want Summer in her life. She didn't need a live-in friend. Diana preferred her privacy. There was nothing wrong with liking to be alone. Just because Mallory couldn't stand quiet, just because Mallory couldn't handle being by herself and had to rush off at every opportunity to meet her fans didn't mean Diana was some kind of freak for liking privacy.

But Mallory hadn't been willing to accept that. She'd imported friendly cousin Summer to replace all the friends Diana had blown off.

"Not that it's Summer's fault," Diana admitted to herself. Summer was all right. It wasn't that.

She got off the highway at the Crab Claw Key exit and drove to the house. Inside, the house was quiet and almost chilly from the air conditioning. The housekeeper had gone home at five, as usual.

Diana parked in the garage and took the kitchen stairs up to her room. At the top of the stairs she froze. Someone was in her room, humming abstractly and pausing occasionally to say, "Ooh, that's beautiful."

Diana took several deep breaths and entered the room. "Excuse me, but what are you doing here?"

Summer jumped and slapped a hand over her heart. "Jeez, you scared me."

"Sorry," Diana said, dripping sarcasm. "I didn't mean to scare you as you went snooping through my closet."

Summer flushed. "I wasn't snooping." She re-hung the dress she'd been admiring. "I was just wondering something."

"Like what?" Diana tossed her purse on her bed and kicked off her sandals.

"I'm supposed to go to this party tonight, and I didn't know what I should wear, so I was looking through your closet to see . . . you know . . ." Her voice petered out. "Sorry, I should have asked first."

"You wanted to *borrow* something to wear?"

"Oh, no, no," Summer said. "No way I'd just borrow something. I just wanted to see if I could figure out what people wear here." She looked embarrassed. The pink flush in her face had become a full-fledged blush.

Diana sighed. "Summer, it doesn't matter what you wear around here. Wear whatever you like."

"That's what she told me too."

"Who?"

"Marquez. Maria Marquez. She says she knows you."

"How on earth did you hook up with Marquez?"

"I met her. She kind of got me a job at the Crab 'n' Conch," Summer said.

Diana's lip curled. "The Cramp and Croak? Good luck."

Summer made a face. "Thanks."

"So what's this about a party?" Diana asked.

Amazing. Summer had been here a day and she had a job, a friend, and an invitation to a party. Getting rid of her had just risen to a new level of difficulty.

"It's at the Merrick estate, this guy named Adam. Oh, wait, you used to go out with him, didn't you?"

Diana nodded slowly. Yes, she had gone out with Adam Merrick.

"Why don't you come too?" Summer said brightly. "Marquez said everyone's invited. I mean, unless you and Adam hate each other or something."

Diana smiled in a way she hoped didn't show too much bitterness. Summer had come very close to the truth. Hate—or something. "No, we don't hate each other," Diana said, working to keep her voice level. "Why would I hate Adam?"

For a brief moment Summer's intelligent, innocent eyes seemed to see past Diana's defenses, seemed to see something hidden just below the surface. Diana looked away, and Summer covered the moment with a laugh.

"I guess I thought when people broke up they couldn't stand to be around each other," Summer said.

"No. Not always," Diana said.

"I could stay home tonight if you wanted to do anything," Summer offered.

"No, no, go to the party. You'll have a good time." Diana felt agitated now, like she needed to escape the room. Get away. "You know, if you want to borrow anything, go right ahead. I have to, uh, I have to take a shower. I spent the whole day shopping."

Diana turned away, fighting the urge to run.

"Diana?"

"What?"

"Are you all right?"

"Just have to go to the bathroom. Is that okay with you?" she snapped suddenly.

"Sure."

"Good." Diana pushed past Summer into her bathroom and closed the door behind her. As an after-thought she turned the lock. Then she turned on the shower and let the water run as hot as she could stand.

She slipped out of her skirt and pulled off the bathing suit underneath and climbed under the stingingly hot spray.

The strength went out of her. She sank to the floor of the shower and sat there, knees drawn up to her chest as the water pounded on her head.

The memories appeared, as she had known they would. Memories of fear and disgust, feelings that made her squirm as if trying to crawl away from her own skin.

Just like that night, when she had come home shaken to her core and sat, just this way, in this very shower, scrubbing herself till she was raw.

9

Frank Has His Say,
and Marquez Has a Very Bad Idea.

Summer left the main house and crossed the sloping lawn to the water's edge. She walked along feeling thoughtful, enjoying the lush grass under her bare feet, wondering about Diana, about the way she had seemed almost panicked.

The little stilt house didn't exactly look like home. Far from it. And yet Summer had a vague, almost affectionate feeling about the place. Not that she had forgotten the sagging bed or the pervasive smell of mildew, but already, after only one day, it felt as if it were hers somehow.

"Aren't I lucky?" she said sardonically.

She crossed the walkway and stopped to slip on the sandals she'd been carrying, stepping over the little piles of bird poop. The pelican—the same pelican, she would have sworn—was sitting on the same corner of the railing, looking her over, its absurdly long beak tucked smugly down.

Summer opened the door and was surprised by the smell. Not the mildew, that was still there, but something new had been added. Fish? Yes, fish.

Fish that was frying in a cast iron skillet on her stove. The bathroom door opened, and out stepped Diver.

He's real! Summer realized in surprise. She'd pretty well convinced herself that Diver was a part of her strange dream the night before. But here he was, still wearing nothing but madras print trunks. Dry, this time. And his hair was dry as well, the ends just touching his broad, deeply tanned shoulders.

"Hey," he said. "You want some fish? I have plenty. He was a big one, so we'd better be eating grouper for the next couple of days."

"What are you doing here?" Summer squealed.

Diver looked nonplussed. "Cooking fish."

"Excuse me, but didn't I explain to you that *I* live here now?"

"I talked to Frank about it. He thinks we should just figure out a way to get along, you know?" Diver used a spatula to turn over first one, then another slab of fish.

"I don't care what Frank said," Summer insisted. "I don't even know any Frank. Who's Frank?"

"Frank. He's outside. This was his place before either of us ever showed up."

"Frank is outside? Where?"

"Out on the railing where he always is," Diver said calmly. "I didn't have anything to make a batter, so I'm just cooking this with some butter. I like it better batter fried, but fresh grouper's good no matter how you cook it. And this boy is fresh. I speared it like an hour ago."

Summer crossed the room to the window and looked outside. She could see most of the railing on that side of the house. The only thing out there was the pelican. Oh. No, that would be crazy, even for someone like Diver.

"Excuse me, but Frank isn't like a bird, is he?"

"A brown pelican," Diver confirmed.

Summer took a deep breath. "You're crazy, aren't you? I mean, no offense, I should probably say . . . sanity challenged or whatever."

Diver looked at her severely. He was holding a spatula and was, Summer had to admit, the best-looking male she'd ever seen in real life. Insane, but devastating.

"*I'm* crazy?" Diver said, as if the idiocy of that statement was self-evident. "Frank's been here since he was hatched, I've been crashing here for like six months, you just show up from Minnesota and tell me to go take a jump, and *I'm* the crazy one? How do you figure that?"

The answer was obvious, Summer knew, only she couldn't think how to express it. "Because my aunt owns this place," she said lamely.

Diver sneered derisively. "Yeah, right. Maybe you should go tell Frank that. Maybe *he'll* care."

"Frank is not the problem," Summer said tersely. "Frank is out there, not in here."

"Duh," Diver said. "He's a bird. Like he'd live in here? This is ready. If you want some, you'd better get a plate."

"Just answer me this," Summer said. "Are you the dangerous kind of insane or the harmless kind?"

Suddenly Diver smiled, a slow, almost shy smile that all by itself answered the question. "I guess I'm more the harmless kind. Only I'm not crazy."

Summer thought about that for a moment. "In Minnesota you'd be crazy."

"This isn't Minnesota," Diver said.

Summer squeezed past him. She grabbed two plates down from the cupboard and two more or less clean forks from the drawer. Then she followed Diver to the small round table.

"I don't need a plate or fork," Diver said. "I'll eat out of the pan."

"Of course," Summer said. "I should have known."

"Shouldn't use stuff you don't need," Diver explained. "Otherwise everything gets used up."

"I agree with that," Summer admitted.

She took a bite of the fish. "Whoa, this is excellent."

"Gotta be fresh, that's the important thing."

Summer watched him eat, watched him use his fingers to gingerly break pieces from the fish in the pan and pop them in his mouth. He didn't look dangerous. If he'd wanted to hurt her, he could have done it the night before. Or now.

Of course, he could still turn out to be nuts. Only . . . there was something about him. Something innocent. So innocent he made Summer feel old and sophisticated. He must have been at least her age, maybe a year or two older. But his eyes held no guile, no secret agenda. He was eating fish and happy doing just that. He believed he could communicate with a big, gray-brown, poop-producing bird.

"I guess you don't have anywhere else to live, huh?" Summer asked him.

He shook his head. "Sometimes I sleep on the beach, but the cops don't like that."

"Is your family from around here?"

He shook his head and formed that embarrassed, shy smile. "I'm the whole family."

"How can that be? You must have some kind of family somewhere."

"I don't know," he mumbled around a piece of fish.

"Okay, let me ask you this. Do you have any clothes? I mean, besides your bathing suit?"

"I have this shirt . . . somewhere." He glanced around as if it might be somewhere nearby.

Mom and Dad would kill you, Summer, if they knew what you were thinking.

Too bad. Mom and Dad were far away. Even Aunt Mallory wasn't there, so it was kind of up to her. "Okay, look, you have to swear to me that you won't get weird on me," Summer said. "I mean, any *more* weird."

His clear, simple gaze met hers. "Okay."

"Swear."

"I swear I won't weird out."

"Okay, then you can stay. We'll have to make up some rules, I guess, but I don't have time right now. I'm supposed to go to a party pretty soon. The only rule I have right now is that no one else can know about you, because if my aunt found out she'd probably ship me back to my parents, who would take turns killing me and grounding me until the middle of the next century."

"Cool. If you come home late, try not to make a lot of noise, all right? It gets Frank all upset."

"Frank."

"Yeah."

"Diver, can I ask you . . . why do you call him Frank?"

Diver shrugged. "It's his name."

Footsteps on the deck outside and a knock on the door.

Summer froze. Her first panicked thought had been that somehow, by some unknown psychic means, her parents had found out and been instantly transported down to Florida.

"Hey, you in there, Summer?"

Summer relaxed. Marquez. Then she *un*relaxed. The party. Was it that late already?

"Coming!" she yelled. "That's my friend—you have to hide," she told Diver.

"No problem, I'm outta here." In a flash he was down the hatchway.

Summer went to the door. Marquez was wearing

skin-tight black shorts and a bright floral bikini top.

"Hey, girl," Marquez said, looking around curiously.

"Hi. I didn't realize it was so late," Summer said. "Pretty impressive place, huh? All the mildew you'll ever need."

"It's very unique," Marquez said, sounding sincere. "I mean, I've seen this place before, of course, but I've never been inside. Are those Jet Skis downstairs?"

"Yes. Too bad I have no idea how to ride them. By the way, you want some fish? I, uh, cooked some."

"I noticed, no offense," Marquez said. "You get to use those Jet Skis?"

"I can if I want, only, like I said, I don't know how."

"Easy to learn. I'll teach you."

"That would be excellent, someday. I just have to brush my teeth real quick and then we can go," Summer said.

"Uh-huh," Marquez said. "You know, Summer . . ."

"What?" Summer answered from the bathroom.

"Well, I don't have a car, my brother's using it, and it's kind of a long walk over to the Merrick estate; you have to go all the way around, it's like two miles unless we get lucky and someone I know comes by."

"That's okay, I can use the exercise," Summer said, trying to talk without dribbling toothpaste. Her mind was leaping back and forth from the impossible notion that she'd let a completely unknown guy practically share her house to the equally impossible concept that she was on her way to party at the Merrick estate.

"Of course, if we went by water across the bay, it would be much shorter." Marquez laughed. "Shorter and a lot more exciting."

Something about Marquez's slightly evil laugh grabbed Summer's attention. "Across the bay? How could we do that?"

"Of course I know how to ride a Jet Ski," Marquez said. "I've lived here in the Keys all my life."

Summer stood beside her on the little platform under the house. It was dark and a bit creepy, with the tar-coated pilings all around and the sense that the house, the entire house, might just decide to fall on their heads at any moment. She looked around, wondering where Diver had gone after running down here. He was nowhere to be seen.

"You don't know how to ride them, do you?" Summer asked, not at all convinced.

"I've *seen* people ride them," Marquez said. "And I know how to drive a car, right, so how different can it be?"

"Well, these go on water is one thing."

Marquez knelt and pried up the seat on the first Jet Ski. Beneath it was a little waterproof locker. "See, just stick your purse and your dress in here, no problem."

Summer pulled the other Jet Ski toward her, a move that involved leaning way out over the water, holding on to a greasy piling and hoping she didn't fall in. The Jet Ski was tied loosely by two ropes and came easily within reach. Summer put her rolled-up dress and purse in the compartment under the seat. At Marquez's insistence she had put on a bathing suit.

"Okay, now we just get on them," Marquez said.

"Marquez, are we going to get ourselves killed?"

"Summer, you need to have more faith. I've seen total morons riding these things, and we're not total morons."

"Not *total*," Summer admitted.

Marquez climbed gingerly onto her Jet Ski. She sat down and gripped the handlebars. "See?"

"Why am I letting you talk me into this?" Summer muttered.

"It will be fun. It'll be cool. You'll see."

Summer climbed on the Jet Ski, which reacted to her weight by wallowing around and spinning slowly away from the platform. Her feet were in the water, but to her amazement the water was perfectly warm, almost hot.

"Okay, see this loop thing?" Marquez called out. "It's just hanging there. You put the loop over your wrist and then you stick the pointy end in here."

"Why?"

"'Cause you need that to start it."

"Why don't they just use a key, like normal machines?"

"See, because this way if you were to fall off, the loop stays on your wrist and that pulls out the pin

77

thing so the Jet Ski stops and doesn't go running off out into the Gulf of Mexico and end up in Haiti."

"Are you sure this is going to be fun?"

"Absolutely. Okay, now to start it, I think you push this button, this green button. And if you want it to go, you press on this red button with your thumb."

Marquez pressed the starter button. The Jet Ski engine coughed and sputtered. She pressed it again, and the engine roared to life. "Nothing to it!" Marquez yelled.

Summer was beginning to get a sick feeling in the pit of her stomach, the feeling she often got when she knew she was doing something not exactly intelligent. But Marquez was enthusiastic, gunning her engine loudly, and the enthusiasm was contagious.

Summer started her own engine, feeling the unfamiliar vibrations through the soles of her bare feet and up through her spine.

"Okay, it started!" she yelled to Marquez.

"Better go slow till we're out from under here," Marquez suggested. She pressed her throttle button and the Jet Ski moved forward. Then it stopped, straining against the rope.

"I think maybe you should untie your rope!" Summer shouted, grinning. Now she was getting caught up in it. They were going to arrive at the fabulous Merrick estate on roaring Jet Skis like a couple of modern mermaids. Much cooler than showing up on foot, all worn out from the walk.

Marquez cast off her rope, and Summer did likewise.

"Real slow, now," Marquez cautioned. She eased her Jet Ski away, carefully guiding it through the pilings.

Summer pressed her own throttle button. The Jet Ski reared and plunged like an out-of-control horse, and then, in a blur, it was roaring through the narrow pilings.

Summer took her finger off the throttle. She was several dozen yards out in the water, well clear of the house. She realized she was shaking and trying very hard not to admit to herself that her head had missed a low beam by two inches at most.

"That's what you call slow?" Marquez said, coming alongside.

"I think I pressed too hard. Now what?"

Marquez pointed across the bay. "Straight across to the other side. It's only maybe half or a third of a mile."

Summer grinned. Now that she had survived the first part, the rest felt like it would be easy. She pressed the throttle again, a bit more carefully, and aimed for the far shore. The Jet Ski roared off with Marquez close alongside.

It was the most exhilarating thing Summer had ever done. The Jet Ski seemed to fly, skimming over the surface of the water, hopping from ripple to ripple, sending up a shower of spray in all directions that soon had Summer drenched, hair flying in the hot breeze.

She glanced back and saw the stilt house silhouetted against a sky turned red by the setting sun.

This was why she had come to Crab Claw Key. This very moment. This sense of being in a new place, doing new things with new people. This overpowering, exhilarating feeling of perfect freedom in the middle of a perfect world.

Soon they were far out in the bay, and the tiny waves let the Jet Skis go airborne, taking off from the slopes of a swell, coming clear out of the water before slapping down again and surging forward.

Then the engine coughed. Speed fell away. The Jet Ski wallowed heavily, power gone. Marquez pulled alongside, idling her engine. She looked as exhilarated as Summer felt, her dark curly hair wild, her eyes lit up.

"What are you doing?"

Summer pushed the starter button. A rasping sound. "I don't know. It just stopped." She tried the starter again. More rasping, a sputter, a rasp.

"Try it again," Marquez suggested.

"Oh no. Is this the gas gauge?" Summer tapped the glass on a small gauge. It read empty. It read less than empty.

Then Marquez's engine sputtered and died. Sudden silence, except for the lapping of water against the Jet Skis. A very ominous silence, the silence of vast, open seas.

"Yep. That's the gas gauge," Marquez said. "Mine says empty."

"Mine agrees," Summer said.

10

Lifestyles of the Rich and Sexy

"A mazing sunset," Summer said. And it was. High streaky clouds appeared in colors that looked too bright and intense to be real. The sun was a ball of brilliant orange-yellow, just peeking above the horizon, threatening to dive into the Gulf of Mexico at any moment. To the east the sky was already darkening. "Incredible," Summer said. "I'm glad I got to experience it before I get washed out to sea and end up being eaten by sharks."

"Someone is bound to see us," Marquez said. "I mean, boats pass in and out of the bay all the time."

"They do? *All* the time?"

"Well, not right now, this minute, but soon. Probably."

They had tied the two Jet Skis together by looping the armholes of Summer's dress over the two sets of handlebars. The dress was getting badly stretched in the process. Now, even if they did make it somehow, she would be arriving at a cool party at a billionaire's estate dressed as clown girl.

The water was still warm, unnaturally warm, like bathwater after it sat for ten minutes. The current was definitely drawing them slowly out of the bay, out toward the open Gulf.

"Maybe we'd better just swim for it," Marquez suggested.

"Great. And how do I explain to Diana and my aunt that on my second day here I brilliantly lost two Jet Skis?"

"Good point," Marquez allowed. "Your aunt might not be happy about that."

"Too bad I have to die this way," Summer said philosophically. "I was just starting to think I might like it here."

"You have a better way to die?" Marquez wondered, making conversation.

"Better would be about eighty years from now."

"Yes. Okay."

"My parents will be upset," Summer said. "It took a lot for them to decide to let me come down here."

"Oh. So they're the very protective type, huh? Mine too."

"I wouldn't say they're *over*protective or anything," Summer said, not sure of how much she should tell Marquez. After all, they'd known each other barely half a day, and so far what Marquez had done was help her get a job, only to turn around and lure her to a watery grave. "They lost my little brother already," Summer said at last. "I mean, I guess he'd be my big brother, but I never think of him that way."

"Oh, man, Summer. I'm sorry to hear that," Marquez said.

"It was a long time ago. I was still a fetus at the time, so naturally I don't remember anything about him. He was two years old and disappeared. I've seen pictures of him. That's all."

"What do you mean, disappeared?"

Summer shrugged. She shouldn't have brought it up. The situation they were in was depressing enough. "He was at day care, playing outside in the yard, and then, suddenly he wasn't. They never found, you know, a body or anything, but after a long, long time my parents finally gave up and accepted it. I don't mean *accepted*. You know what I mean."

"That's very major, Summer. That's horrible." Marquez whistled softly in the dark. "I wouldn't have thought you were someone with any kind of sadness in your life, you know? You seem so sweet and normal and all."

For a while they were both silent, listening to the plop of fish jumping out of the water. It had been a long time since Summer had thought much about the brother she'd never known. When she was younger, the sadness of that one event had hung over every day. It was a sadness that had been there, waiting for her as she was born into the world.

"Summer, you're not crying, are you? It's so dark I can't really see your face. I hate tears."

"No," Summer lied. "It was something that happened before I was even born. You can't be sad over things that happen before you're born."

The sun had finally plunged below the horizon, taking the last of the optimism with it. Darkness moved swiftly toward them across the water. Over on the shore a few hundred yards away they could see the lights of the party, an impression of people moving back and forth under the trees, the head-lights of cars pulling up.

"Hey, there's a light," Summer said, wiping away the tears that blurred her vision. It was a green pinpoint of light moving fast.

"It's a boat," Marquez said excitedly, confirming Summer's faint hope.

"Hey!" Summer yelled. "Hey, boat! Help! Do you think he sees us?"

"Jeez, I hope so. I don't want to die out here," Marquez said.

"I thought you weren't worried," Summer accused.

"I didn't want to worry you."

"HELP!"

"HELP US! HELP, you blind—"

"He's coming. I think." Summer could hear the sound of the boat's engines, deep and powerful and reassuring. The boat was definitely coming closer. In fact, it had just begun to occur to Summer that the boat might hit them. But then it slowed, in-scribing a slow circle around them. A spotlight played across the dark water and illuminated them, two insanely waving figures.

"That you, Marquez?" a mocking voice called out.

"Adam?" Marquez yelled back. "What took you so long?"

"We saw you out here, but we didn't believe it was possible for two Jet Skis to break down at the same exact time."

"We ran out of gas," Marquez said.

The boat, very long and very fast-looking with two big outboard engines, drifted alongside. There were two guys in the boat. Even in the darkness Summer could see the resemblance between them. They looked like brothers.

One dived over the side of the boat and surfaced between the two Jet Skis, spouting water and laughing. He was carrying a white nylon rope. "We'll tow you in, ladies. Let me just tie this . . ." He fell silent, looking up at Summer, who was sitting on her Jet Ski in a damp pink bikini, feeling like the biggest dweeb in recorded history.

"Hi," he said. He stuck a hand up to her. She shook it briefly, but he held on for an extra second, making contact. "I'm Adam Merrick. In the boat there is my brother, Ross."

"Pleased, et cetera," said a voice from the boat. A voice that sounded as if it had been affected by a few beers.

"Thanks for rescuing us," Summer said, her voice a little squeaky.

"What's a nice girl like you doing with Marquez? I'll bet you ten bucks this was all *her* idea, right?" Adam said.

"Hey," Marquez said, pushing Adam underwater with her foot. "What makes you think it was my idea?"

"I *know* you, Marquez," Adam said.

"This is Summer. She's from Idaho or Michigan or one of those places," Marquez said.

"Minnesota. Bloomington. You know, the Mall of America?" Excellent, Summer chided herself. Absolutely mention the Mall of America. That's sure to impress a billionaire who has probably been all over the world ten times.

"Guess whose cousin she is?" Marquez asked.

"Cindy Crawford's?" Adam suggested. He released Summer's hand and began looping the rope to the towing rings in the front of each Jet Ski.

"Summer is Diana's cousin," Marquez said. "Diana Olan."

Adam said nothing. From the boat came Ross's unpleasant laugh. "Let's leave her out here."

"Shut up, Ross," Adam snapped. He forced a smile for Summer. An apologetic and extraordinarily attractive smile. A movie star smile. "Come on, get in the boat."

"Okay," Summer said. Marquez made the jump easily from her Jet Ski to the boat, swinging over the side and brushing her hands together as if she'd just done a neat trick.

Summer stood up and reached for the side of the boat. But the Jet Ski slid away. She plunged into the water. It closed over her head, surprising her and frightening her a little. She wasn't a great swimmer, though she could stay afloat. But this was open sea, and it was dark, and the music from *Jaws* had already been running through the back of her mind.

With a kick she headed for a surface dappled and rippling with reflected light.

Then there were powerful arms around her, holding her firmly. They broke the surface. Her face was inches from Adam's, and the first thought that popped into her mind was that she probably didn't look great right then, water streaming off her head, spitting out seawater. Whereas Adam definitely did look great, wet or not. Her hands felt hard muscle in his neck. Her breasts were pressed against his chest, close enough that she could feel his every breath.

"You okay?" Adam asked. She could feel the rumble of his voice.

"I'm fine. I *can* swim, you know."

"That's good. Swimming is important around here."

"Yeah. You can, um, let me go now."

"Do I have to?" Adam asked.

Marquez leaned over the side, offering Summer a hand. Summer took it and pulled hard but was unable to clear the drag of the water entirely. Then there were hands firmly planted on her behind, pushing her up.

She slid over the side of the boat and gasped out her embarrassed thanks. Adam pulled himself up and over, an almost effortless move. He sat beside her and leaned across her to reach a cabinet. He found two towels and handed one to her.

"Thanks," Summer mumbled.

"My extreme pleasure," Adam said. "It's hot," he added quickly, as if he realized he'd sounded slightly sleazy. "Too hot, and a dive in the water was just what I needed."

He even seemed sincere, Summer thought. But then again, he was from a political family. They probably had special genes that gave them the ability to sound sincere.

"All right, enough of playing Coast Guard, back to the party," Ross said.

The boat moved along slowly, careful not to swamp the two Jet Skis bobbing along behind. If Ross was drunk, he still seemed able to pilot the boat, berthing it neatly alongside the dock.

"I'm not exactly dressed for a party anymore," Summer pointed out, indicating her bathing suit. The dress she had planned to wear was a total loss.

"There'll be plenty of girls wearing smaller bathing suits than that," Adam assured her.

Marquez nodded, and Summer began to wonder whether this was the kind of party she wanted to attend. But Marquez gave her a reassuring wink and a little shake of the head that said, hey, don't worry about it.

"Stay," Adam said. "Please."

Again he sounded as if he really wanted her to stay. As if she was supposed to believe that someone like Adam Merrick really cared one way or the other if some tourist from the home of the Mall of America went to his party.

"Okay, I guess. Thanks." There was no polite way to get out of it. Not now. She didn't even know the way home.

A neat, crushed-shell path led from the dock across a vast lawn toward the house. It was painful under Summer's tender feet, so she walked onto the grass, as thick and spongy as a mattress.

The house was just two stories high, but it extended in every direction, looking as large as the main building of Summer's high school. Some, if not most, of the windows were bright, revealing strangely positioned cupolas and parapets and sudden, capricious balconies.

But the party wasn't in the house. The party was in front of the house, past the looping driveway crammed with cars, past the naked, spotlit flagpole. Summer could see a mass of bodies writhing under the reddish light of Japanese lamps hung from the trees, long hair flying in time with the music, arms randomly thrust into the air, smooth, tan female legs everywhere, protruding from shorts and minis and bathing suit bottoms. Hairy guy legs as well, looking stubby in big shorts or extremely long in little European bathing suits.

Ross disappeared into the throng, but Adam stayed close, following Summer onto the grass. As they reached the driveway he strode ahead, walking with an easy grace and absolute confidence. Nothing exaggerated or forced, no swagger, no attempt to impress anyone, just a walk that announced him as the guy in charge, at home and utterly sure of himself.

Summer was just behind him, feeling simultaneously invisible and horribly conspicuous, like a stagehand who had wandered into the star's spotlight.

The sound system was playing 2Pac, and when Summer glanced over her shoulder, she saw that Marquez was already dancing. The beat seemed to reach across the distance and grab control of Marquez's body. She was dancing over the crushed shell, turning the gravel into her own muted rhythm section.

Around the fringes of the dancing little knots of people could be seen, here and there, faces appearing in the dim glow of a cigarette. Other groups were smaller, usually just two bodies pressed close, making out as they leaned against tree trunks or against the hoods of the nearest cars.

Summer had begun to feel increasingly nervous as she got closer to the party. The music was familiar; the dancing, too. Even the wafting smells of beer and smoke weren't much different from parties back home. But usually when she went to parties, she knew at least half the people there. Knew whom she could hang out with, which guys she could dance with, how to say no to the various offers of one kind or another. Here she was a stranger. The only person she knew at all was Marquez, and Marquez seemed to have been possessed by the music.

Ross Merrick took Marquez by the arm and led her away into the melee. "Have fun," Marquez called back to Summer.

And then Summer was alone, the instant loser,

the one on the fringe with no one to talk to. Except for Adam, who was still there, close by, though he was fielding a steady stream of hellos, hey dudes, and congratulations on the excellence of the party. But the last thing she wanted was to be Adam's pity date, someone to be handed off at the earliest opportunity.

"Want to dance?" Adam asked.

The request shouldn't have surprised her—this *was* a party—and yet it did.

Dance? In a wet two-piece bathing suit? With this guy she'd barely met? This guy she'd seen on the news once, standing in a group with his famous father? But what was the alternative to dancing? Standing around gaping at people?

"Sure," Summer said, half-grateful, half-frightened. What were the chances that her bathing suit bottom would bunch up while she was dancing?

Adam took her hand and drew her to what Summer could now see was an actual dance floor: interlocked, polished wood planks laid out on the grass. Here and there portions were raised so that some dancers were elevated above the rest.

The sound system played a Young M.C. tune, and Summer began to dance, intensely conscious of what she felt must be many alien eyes on her. Although each time she glanced around she never saw anyone staring at her, it was hard to shake the feeling that the eyes were there.

"So you're Diana's cousin," Adam said, drawing close alongside her, shouting a little to be heard. He even danced well.

"Uh–huh." Summer was concentrating, trying to remember the moves she'd seen girls doing on that MTV beach show, trying to stay in time with the beat.

"Just down here for the summer. For the summer, Summer?" He grinned. "I guess you've heard that joke about a million times."

Summer smiled and shrugged. A mistake, since shrugging upset her carefully maintained rhythm, and her legs and arms and head now were each off doing different things, as if listening to three different songs.

"How do you like it so far?" Adam asked. "Crab Claw Key, I mean."

"It's beautiful," Summer said. Was the tie on her bathing suit top coming loose? No. No, but she'd double the knot when she got the chance.

"Just beautiful?" Adam said, sounding disappointed.

"It's . . . different. I mean, it's like . . . it's like there aren't any real adults, you know? No one wears a suit or looks serious about anything."

Adam laughed. "That's exactly right. No adults. Even people seventy years old aren't adults here."

"Also I feel like people here are stranger, more out–there, you know?" Summer suggested, thinking of Diver—definitely strange. And Marquez—probably strange. And Seth, who was only strange if you thought putting a lip lock on a total stranger in a photo booth was unusual.

"Everything is a little more extreme," Adam

agreed. "Back home I'm a totally different person."

"Home? Don't you live here?"

"No, this is mostly just a summer home. We're from New Hampshire. I spend about a third of the year here between all the vacations, summer and spring and weekends."

"Oh, that's right, how stupid of me, duh. Your father is the senator from New Hampshire, obviously."

Adam looked pained. "You're not into politics, are you?"

"Not exactly," Summer admitted. "I mean, I was secretary-treasurer of my tenth-grade class, but we never had any meetings and there wasn't any money." Is it even possible for me to sound like a bigger idiot? Secretary-treasurer of the tenth grade?

"You have a boyfriend?" Adam asked, suddenly shifting course. He smiled. The music assumed a slower, more sultry beat. Couples danced closer together. Janet Jackson, "Any Time, Any Place." Summer recognized the song. Suddenly she had a very clear image of the video for that song. She hadn't seen it in months, but now, at a very inconvenient time, she could recall far too many images.

"No, I don't really have a boyfriend," Summer admitted. Sure, I have this guy I make out with in airports who has a girlfriend, and this other guy who lives with me but doesn't like girls, but no, no actual boyfriends.

They danced for a while, with Adam drawing closer, matching his rhythm to hers. He was a good dancer, graceful for a guy so large. Graceful and smooth and confident, and like some kind of a sun, so that she could feel the force of gravity drawing her toward him.

At least his bathing suit was normal, not like the little Speedos some of the guys were wearing. "Well, aren't you going to ask *me?*" he said after a while.

"Ask you what?" Summer said, alarmed.

"Ask me if I have a girlfriend."

"Um . . ."

"I don't," Adam said, grinning impishly.

"Oh." Summer gulped. What was she supposed to say now? "I can't believe you don't have a girlfriend?" Or "Cool, can I be your girlfriend?" Or what? He seemed to think she should say *something*.

"I've never really had a boyfriend," Summer said. Instantly, even as the words were bubbling out of her mouth, she wished she could call them back. Too late. And now her brain became totally useless, because Adam was dancing *very* close, and the pictures from the Janet Jackson video were *very* clear in Summer's mind, and so was the memory of his arms around her in the water. "I mean, not a real boyfriend, not that I don't like guys because I do, it's just that the guys who . . . I mean, the wrong guys and then the right guys were, you know, and . . ." She was in full babble mode now. Words totally unconnected to any sensible thought were spewing forth, unstoppable. Full babble. Total brain lock that shut down her mind and her body so that now her dancing had deteriorated into spasms of random muscle jerks.

She was dancing in a bikini with the very attractive son of a billionaire senator and doing her best impression of a moron having a seizure.

"Oh, man," Adam said, peering over Summer's head. "The butler's calling to me."

Thank God. Just go away and leave me to my humiliation.

"I have to go see what he wants," Adam said.

He almost sounded like he was honestly regretful, Summer noted. Although clearly he was just grabbing the first excuse to escape her. Flee, Adam, flee! Run from the dweeb girl. Run before she can mention the Mall of America again. "Okay," Summer said gratefully.

"Um, before I go, though . . ." Adam said. "There's just one thing I wanted to clear up."

"What? Um, what would you . . . what?"

"Well, around here we have this custom. When someone rescues someone, like I rescued you out on the bay, well, there's this customary thing."

"Okay," Summer said cautiously.

"The rescuer gets to kiss the person he rescued."

Before Summer had a chance to object—and she wasn't sure whether she planned to—Adam had put his arm around her and drawn her close. There was a last split second when she could have said no, but then the split second was gone.

Adam's lips met hers. Only for an instant. Then he pulled away, still keeping his hold on her. "Don't disappear on me," he said in a low voice. "I'll be right back."

11

Hot Music and Sweaty Bodies, a Long Way from Minnesota

I saw that," Marquez said, sounding almost accusatory. "I bring you to a party and the first thing you do is throw yourself at the host? Bad girl. *Bad* girl. Shame." Then she broke up, laughing gaily at the horrified expression on Summer's face.

"I didn't throw myself at him. I hardly know him," Summer protested anxiously. Kissing people *she* hardly knew was getting to be a habit.

"Whatever." Marquez waved her hand. "So, how was it?"

"I didn't even know it was happening."

That really started Marquez giggling. "Well, I guess you're off to a good start, huh? Practically your first night out and Adam Merrick is all over you."

"I don't think it meant anything," Summer said doubtfully.

"He kissed you. That had to mean something.

96

Adam isn't a total dirtbag who runs around kissing girls. Unless he's gotten worse since last summer. You know, someday he may be senator or governor. Or president."

"He used to go out with my cousin," Summer pointed out. The thought had just occurred to her, probably because her mind was just coming out of brain lock.

"Ancient history," Marquez said. "Come on, you don't want to hang around looking like you're waiting for him."

"I'm *not* waiting. I don't even know him."

"Yeah, yeah. Either way you don't want to just stand here, do you?"

"No, I guess not."

"Come on, let's dance."

"The two of us?"

"I have to dance," Marquez said, as if that were obvious. "And I don't see any guys asking either of us right this minute. Besides, they're starting to play some better music. Rap is cool, but I feel like totally thrashing out with some serious rock."

From the speakers the Ramones began roaring through "I Wanna Be Sedated." For Marquez, the transition from standing around to dancing was instantaneous and total. It wasn't about looking cool, it was about losing all contact with the normal world, going away to a place where her body and mind and the music were all the same thing.

It was impossible for Summer to resist. Impossible not to be drawn in. The night was hot, and Marquez was dancing like someone possessed, and Summer could still feel Adam's lips on hers, could still recall the shock when his arm had gone around her in the water and the contact of flesh against flesh.

She had just been kissed by a guy. Kissed by a very cute guy, and she wanted to be kissed again.

As long as it didn't turn out that Adam had his own Lianne hidden away somewhere.

The music throbbed through her as Marquez guided them toward the speakers like a moth drawn to a candle, louder and louder till the music wasn't a sound anymore but something that came from inside her.

She'd been kissed by a complete stranger, and she had liked it. Held by a guy she didn't know and had liked that too. And worst of all, it was the second time in less than a week. Ha! Try calling *that* "nice."

The *nice* Summer Smith was dead and lying in her grave while the new, improved, bolder, wilder, goes-to-parties, kisses-guys-she-hardly-knows Summer Smith shoveled dirt over her.

Summer closed her eyes and danced.

When she opened her eyes again Adam was there, as if in answer to a wish. He smiled and she smiled back. She closed her eyes again, afraid that looking at him she might feel the edge of self-awareness return, the sense of eyes following her, judging her.

With her eyes closed Summer had the feeling that she could dance like Marquez. She'd forgotten that she was surrounded by strangers and was dancing in a two-piece bathing suit. She felt drunk, though she'd had nothing to drink. She peeked from under narrowed lids as Adam danced closer, so that now she could reach out and touch him if she wanted to, touch his smooth chest.

The music slowed from its exhausting pace into a gentler but still intoxicating reggae song. This, at last, was the right music, she thought. The melody of sunbaked islands and warm nights and people who never, ever wore parkas.

Summer realized they were no longer on the floor. There was grass under her feet as she danced, and the music, though still loud, had softened a little. It was darker now, and Adam was closer. Inches separated them, and his eyes were focused on hers. She looked down, embarrassed, but this time she didn't feel like being embarrassed, so she looked up and met his gaze.

The music paused between songs. Summer felt something rough at her back and leaned against the tree. Adam came closer.

"You are very, very beautiful," Adam said. He made no attempt to hide the fact that his eyes were taking in her entire body. "Are you sure you don't have a boyfriend?"

"I'm sure," Summer said, her voice a distant, Minnie Mouse squeak.

Adam leaned first one hand and then the other against the tree, imprisoning her.

Now would be the time to say, "Hey, hold up, I

barely know you," Summer told herself. Yes, now would be the time. Right now, before he leaned any closer.

This time when he kissed her it wasn't the quick, almost playful kiss she'd felt earlier. This time he really kissed her. And the music started up again, soft but insistent. He kissed her and to her utter amazement, Summer kissed him back.

Something hit Summer on her right side. She staggered and nearly tripped over a body.

"Whoa, sorry." A guy scrambled up, standing awkwardly in the very small space between Summer and Adam. "I tripped. Over a root or something. Adam, dude, you ought to talk to your gardener about that. A guy could get killed."

"You been drinking, Mr. Moon?" Adam asked, taking a step back.

Summer peered through the darkness. Yes, it *was* Seth. *Seth!* Possibly the last person on earth she wanted to see right at this moment. What was he doing here?

"Hey, it's Summer," Seth said. "Summer from Minnesota."

"Hi. Again," Summer said. For reasons she couldn't immediately explain, she felt guilty. Feeling guilty just made her feel angry.

Seth smiled a little lopsidedly. "So, I see you're getting to know people, making friends and all." He rolled his eyes exaggeratedly at Adam.

"Good-bye, Seth," Adam said tersely. "Great seeing you again, welcome anytime and so on."

"I was just going to ask Summer to dance," Seth said.

"She's busy."

"That's very disappointing." Seth shrugged.

Suddenly a new sound mixed in with the music, then rose louder still. Shouting, one voice loudly enraged and other voices trying to instill calm. Summer saw a disturbance on the far side of the dance floor.

"Sounds like Ross has gone off again," Seth said, not unkindly.

Adam bit his lip and glanced uncertainly at Summer.

"Go on, deal with it," Seth said to Adam. "Don't worry, I'm not going to take her anywhere."

The noise was beginning to sound like a fight, with shouts of encouragement from at least two sides.

Adam cursed. "I'll be back. Don't let Mr. Moon here give you any crap."

"What's happening?" Summer asked Seth.

Seth shrugged. "Oh, Ross is drunk and picking fights. Drunk or high, or maybe E: all of the above."

"Adam's brother?"

"Yeah. It happens." Seth looked uncomfortable. "So, um, sorry if I broke anything up. Not *real* sorry, though."

"I'm not sorry," Summer said before she'd had a chance to think about it. "Not that . . . I mean . . ." She sighed. "Forget it."

"Okay. Forgotten. So, you want to dance? It looks like the fight is getting under control. Besides, it's way over there."

"I don't know if I should dance any more," Summer said. She felt as if she were coming out of a trance. It was a disturbing feeling, like thinking you'd been talking in your sleep and wondering what people might have heard.

"Take it slow, Minnesota," Seth said kindly. "You know, all this down here gets to people sometimes. Warm nights, ocean breezes in the palm trees, that whole tropical thing . . . you might just forget who you are. Forgetting who you are is the whole idea of Crab Claw Key."

Summer blushed. "I did not forget who I was," she said. She said it with extra conviction because it wasn't true. "And unlike certain people, I don't forget I have a girlfriend I've been going with for four years."

Seth winced. "Look, what I told you was true— I *did* break up with Lianne. Only . . . I guess she doesn't want to accept it."

"Poor you," Summer said sarcastically. "I guess she can't give you up because you're just so wonderful. And you say *I'm* the one who's forgetting who they are?"

Seth nodded glumly. "Yeah, I guess I deserved that. Okay. Cool. I'm just saying look out for that tropical effect, that tropical rot. It eats away at everything, so that things here deteriorate faster, fall apart faster, and then it all grows back faster and wilder than before. The old stuff disappears." He snapped his fingers. "And before you know it, something new has shot up overnight to take its place."

"I'm a grown person," Summer said sharply. "I think I can make my own decisions."

Seth pulled off his cap and made an exaggerated bow. "I apologize. None of my business."

"That's right, *none* of your business," Summer said.

He started to walk away, then he turned back. "Just for your information, I didn't lie to you."

Summer met his gaze, and suddenly she was back in the airport, with his mouth on hers, feeling a surge of something she'd never felt before that moment.

He looked as if he was telling the truth. His eyes didn't waver or turn away.

Adam had asked her to wait for him. Seth was drawing her closer with just his gaze. . . .

Suddenly there was a loud, feminine squeal. A look of confusion clouded Seth's face, then was quickly replaced by dread or embarrassment or both.

"Sethie!" the voice squealed again.

"Lianne?" he said in a whisper.

A girl appeared, running joyfully, arms outstretched like something from a slow-motion movie. She was short, but with that uniquely petite perfection. Pale, almost translucent skin. Dark red hair that fell over her shoulders in a luxuriant wave. She was wearing shorts and a cropped top.

She leapt on Seth, wrapping her bare legs around his waist, her arms around his neck. He supported her minimal weight by linking his hands beneath her bottom.

"Are you surprised?" Lianne asked gleefully. "I decided to come down a few days early. I just couldn't stand to be separated a minute longer."

She kissed him, a peck on each cheek, then a long, slow kiss.

It may have been that Seth was trying to push her away. It may have been that he tried to avoid her kisses. But Summer had seen enough. She turned on her heel and walked away.

At a safe distance, from under the dark shadows of the trees, she looked back. Seth and Lianne were standing close, deep in conversation. Then Seth turned and walked a short distance. He hesitated. Summer saw his shoulders sag.

Lianne went to him and looked up at his face. A red lantern was just above them, and it cast a shadowy pink light on Lianne's pretty features.

Lianne put her arms around Seth. His arms hung limp. And then, just barely tall enough to look over Seth's shoulder, Lianne aimed her gaze directly at Summer. It was impossible at that distance to read her expression.

Summer shrank back against the nearest tree trunk. Lianne couldn't possibly see her even there in the dark, could she?

And yet, for just a fleeting moment, despite the hot night, Summer felt a chill.

She spotted Seth a few times after that, drinking soda, talking to people, dancing a little with Lianne and other girls. But he said nothing to Summer.

And Summer said nothing to him. She didn't care about Seth Warner. And now, she assured herself, she would be able to put the airport incident behind her for good.

She was wandering around on the steps leading up to the main door of the estate house, hoping for a clue to the nearest bathroom, when she ran into Adam.

"*There* you are," Adam said, appearing at the bottom of the stone steps. He was wearing a shirt now, and he looked subdued.

"Hi," she said.

"Were you looking for me?" Adam asked.

Summer hesitated and Adam laughed. "I guess not," he said ruefully.

"I was sort of looking for a bathroom, but I'd rather find you," she said hastily. She winced. "I don't think that came out exactly the way I meant it."

"You meant I was second runner-up behind a bathroom. That's okay," he said. "I can live with that. Come on."

He trotted up the stairs and took her hand. He led her to the door and used a key to unlock it. "We usually just let the party guests use the bathrooms by the pool house. I have to keep the doors of the main house locked or Manolo will kill me. He's the butler, all-around guy in charge of the house. He's the *real* boss."

They entered an arched atrium and set off down a long hallway. It was like stepping directly out of Florida and clear across time and space to nineteenth-century New England. The senator's tastes obviously didn't embrace the lighter, looser Florida look. The walls were lined with alternating gilt-framed floor-to-ceiling mirrors and paintings, all more or less gloomy portraits of stern-looking men.

"The Merrick clan," Adam said, noticing her awed expression. "There's a set just like them in the New Hampshire house. All the dead Merrick men. Someday I'll be there too, looking old and serious. That guy there?" He pointed. "That's Aubrey Merrick. He used to import slaves, back in like 1795 or something. He didn't *approve* of slavery, of course, but business was business."

"Wow" was all Summer could think of to say.

"And that guy, the guy with the whiskers, he was cool. He sort of made up for old Aubrey. That's Josiah. He died with the Maine boys on Little Round Top at Gettysburg. Took three bullets and was still yelling and shooting rebels when he keeled over dead."

"I saw that movie," Summer said. Her eyes met Adam's and they both laughed. It was a relief to laugh.

"Someday in the year 2090 or whatever, some young Merrick guy will be walking along with some girl he's trying to impress and point to me. 'That's Adam Merrick. Never did a damned thing.'"

"Maybe you'll do something," Summer said.

Adam smirked. "Yeah, maybe. If they decide to hold another civil war, I'm there."

"And then you'll be in the new movie. Played by Keanu Reeves or someone."

"Do you like Keanu Reeves?" Adam asked.

"Yeah. He's cute, I guess. I mean, um, he's a good actor."

"You know, when you blush like that it makes me want to kiss you again," Adam said.

"I thought you were showing me a bathroom."

"Oh, right." They reached the end of the hallway and entered a vast, open room, two floors high. Rough wood beams, each as big as a full-size tree, supported the ceiling. The walls were paneled in dark wood. The furniture, though there was a lot of it, seemed lost in the space. At one side of the room was a fireplace, fire roaring under a granite mantel that reminded Summer of pictures of Stonehenge.

"You must have the only fireplace in this state," Summer said.

"Certainly the only one in use when it's in the high eighties outside," Adam agreed. "My dad likes fires. So the staff lights it every night, whether he's here or not, no matter how hot it is outside." He laughed. "Seems slightly absurd, right?"

"Maybe. But I'm starting to get the feeling that it takes an awful lot to seem absurd around this place."

Adam laughed his easy laugh. "Ah, you're starting to get the picture. See, I know what you mean. I guess New Hampshire is similar to Minnesota in a lot of ways. It makes you slightly schizo going back and forth between the 'normal' world and this island."

"Seth said something kind of like that," Summer said. She instantly regretted mentioning Seth.

Adam just rolled his eyes slightly. He pointed to

a small door, almost invisible in the paneling. "There you go. At least I think that's a bathroom."

"How many are there in this house?"

"Twenty-one, I think. We have like twenty-six at the New Hampshire house. We thought that many would be too ostentatious for Florida, though." He laughed to show that he was just kidding.

But somehow for Summer, the fact that this one family had a total of forty-seven bathrooms (possibly more because who knew if they owned other houses?) was deeply impressive. Forty-seven bathrooms. Forty-seven rolls of toilet paper. They must buy it in truckloads. Forty-seven little Ty-D-Bols.

When she came back, she found Adam standing a few feet from the fire. It made a dark silhouette of his body, accentuating the heavy shoulders, the muscular torso. Even in silhouette he exuded easy confidence, something bred in him, something that announced to the world that here was a person without self-doubt, without awkwardness, without self-consciousness.

It drew Summer to him, and yet frightened her just a little. He was so different from other guys her own age. He could easily be twenty-five, or even forty.

Maybe being rich made it possible to just sort of glide by all the little tortures of teenagehood. After all, Summer realized, Adam didn't worry about getting work, or getting accepted to college, or paying for college, or whether he could afford to buy cool clothes, or if his folks would get him a car. If he ever got a zit, they probably flew in a whole team of dermatologists to get rid of it.

He noticed her and turned. "Was it a bathroom?"

"No, it was a closet, but I went anyway," she said, and he laughed. She wasn't going to act all impressed and inferior with him. Just because he could probably buy her entire family with his week's allowance.

"Would you like a drink?" he asked.

"I don't drink very much," Summer said.

"That's probably good. Booze is our favorite family vice. I don't drink because it makes me break out in hives." He laughed. "Seriously. It's not a pretty sight."

"I guess I should get back outside and see what Marquez is doing," Summer suggested.

"Marquez can take care of herself." He shook his head slowly, amused. "She's very cool. Just don't ever make her mad. The girl has a temper. One of those ice-cold tempers, you know?"

"She's been really nice to me," Summer said. "Like bringing me here."

"I'm very glad she did that," Adam said.

Summer debated whether to ask the next question. It could ruin things instantly, and her impertinent questions had ruined other relationships before. "Do you try to pick up just any new girl that shows up around here?"

He looked startled. "You mean you think I'm trying to impress you and score with you so that I can add another notch to my belt?"

"I guess that's what I mean," Summer said. "Some guys *are* like that." She could think of at least one by name.

"Maybe I should ask *you* a question. Are you trying to make it with me so that you can tell all your friends you dated Adam Merrick? Or perhaps even go to the *National Enquirer* and sell the story— 'My Hot Affair with Boy Billionaire'?"

Summer recoiled. "Why would you think *that?*"

"It happens," Adam said. "Just like it happens that some guys, whether or not they happen to come from a wealthy family, try to see how many girls they can pick up."

"Oh. I guess you're right. I guess that is true, isn't it?"

"I'll tell you the absolute truth, cross my heart and hope to die. I saw you sitting there, looking lost on that Jet Ski, and I instantly thought 'what an idiot. How could she manage to get stuck out here like this?'"

"That's very flattering."

"Then I jumped in to help you—admittedly I was happy to have an excuse to put my arms around you, since we're being honest here—and . . ." He made a wry face. "And something just happened. It felt like something I wanted to do again. And when you talked, it was this voice that I wanted to hear again. And when you spit seawater out of your mouth, it was a mouth I wanted to kiss. And then I did kiss you, and wanted to kiss you again. Like I do now."

Summer swallowed once. Twice. "We'd better not," she said. "It's all kind of . . . tropical."

"Tropical?"

"I mean, we haven't even had a date or anything."

Adam slapped his forehead. "I knew I'd forgotten something! Would you go out with me? Tomorrow? No, wait, day after tomorrow." He took Summer's hands in his. "Would you go out with me?"

"Yes," Summer said, sounding weirdly stiff. "That would be excellent."

It was about one in the morning when Marquez finally tired out. Half the people at the party had already left, and Marquez found Summer asleep, leaning back against a tree trunk with an empty Mountain Dew in her hand, her now dry but still misshapen dress laid over her like a blanket.

For a moment Marquez considered playing some prank on the gently snoring girl, but she was too weary to think of anything and besides, Summer wasn't a person you could be mean to.

She knelt and shook Summer's arm.

"What?"

"Time to wake up. We should get going. This guy I know with a truck said he'd give us a lift."

"What?" Summer repeated. She was looking around with that confused where-am-I look.

Marquez took her hand and pulled her to her feet. They headed for the driveway, where a battered red pickup truck was idling. In the cab beside the driver were two other guys Marquez knew from school.

"You're going to make us ride in the back?" Marquez asked. "What gentlemen."

"James here is probably going to hurl," the driver pointed out. "You'll be safer in the back."

"Don't say 'hurl,'" a voice groaned.

She and Summer climbed over the tailgate, and Marquez pounded twice on the roof of the truck, signaling the driver that he could go.

They took off down the winding, wooded path through the Merrick estate.

"I didn't say good night to Adam," Summer said.

"Too late now," Marquez said. "Besides, I think he disappeared around midnight with a bunch of guys who said they were going to drive to some club down in Key West."

"Oh."

Marquez rolled her eyes. "If you're going to hang around with Adam Merrick, you have to deal with the fact that he and his buds move kind of fast."

"Oh," Summer said again, nodding vaguely.

"So, you going to see him again?"

"I don't know. I think so. I hope so. He said he'd like to take me out on a real date. You know, dinner and all that. Day after tomorrow."

"You don't sound totally psyched."

"I'm just tired," Summer said. "And it seems unreal, you know? This whole place. All of a sudden I meet a bunch of new people and go to a big party at a senator's house and kiss this guy I barely even met."

"Uh-huh. So, it was good, right?"

Summer giggled unexpectedly. "The first one was too quick, and I didn't even know what was happening. Later we had a longer one. That was kind of nice."

"Kind of nice?" Marquez made a face. "Don't tell that to Adam. He thinks he's the stud prince of planet earth."

"It's not that," Summer said. "It's just that I don't have all that much to compare it to. I mean, half the time I was just scared that I would do something stupid, you know? Like burp or suddenly develop insta-zits. I've never kissed someone famous before."

Marquez smiled. "But how did it make you *feel?*"

Summer nodded her head from side to side and scrunched her face up, struggling for some definition. "It made me feel slightly sick. Like maybe I was getting the flu. Or else like the time I visited my grandmother in Virginia and we went on a roller coaster at King's Dominion. It was my first ever roller coaster, and I felt sick but also giddy and wobbly. It was fun, but I wasn't sure I wanted to go on it again. Do you know what I mean?"

Marquez nodded knowingly. "You'll go on it again."

12

Hi, Jennifer. Sorry I'm whispering, but Diver is asleep up on the roof and I don't want him to hear me. Yes, I know, I need to explain about that. I guess a lot's been happening even though I feel like I just got here.

Anyway, it's almost two o'clock in the morning, but I couldn't fall asleep mostly because I'm kind of excited. I mean, I'm really excited, I guess. You know what happened tonight? This guy kissed me. This guy named Adam. Not Seth. Seth is the other one I told you about, the using creep with a girlfriend.

Forget him. This is Adam I'm talking about now. Totally different situation. I hope.

Now I'm going to tell you his last name, but you have to swear, absolutely swear, you won't tell anyone, and I mean it. Okay. Did you swear?

Adam *Merrick*. You know, like the senator? His

son. They have a house you would not believe. You'd faint if you saw it. It's the size of a castle. Diana's mom's house is like one tenth the size. Anyway, we went to a party there, me and Marquez.

Wait, I haven't told you about Marquez, either. Marquez is this girl I met here. She's very cool and dances really well. Anyway, we're going to this party at the Merrick estate, right? And we fall into the water. I mean, *I* fall into the water, being the klutzoid one. And Adam jumps in and gets me, not that I was drowning or anything, but he didn't know that. So later he says I should let him kiss me because he rescued me, right? So, he did. Just a little kiss, only later we danced and then we ended up making out. For kind of a long time.

It was just like you told me it was with Blake, so now I guess we're equal. Unless you've been doing something you shouldn't, you bad girl. And if you have, you'd better tell me because I'm telling you *everything*.

Except for Diver. Which is complicated. See, he kind of lives here. He's very nice but a little strange. I mean, he thinks he can communicate with Frank, and Frank is a pelican.

I don't know why I'm letting him stay here. He just comes in to use the kitchen or the bathroom, so it's not like he's really living here. Just do not ever tell Mom about this or I'll kill you. I'm serious.

I don't know what I'm doing anymore, Jennifer. It's weird, almost, because it's like I just get here and boom! I'm kissing this guy in a photo booth at the airport, and then boom! I have this other guy practically living in my house, and then boom! I'm at a party making out with Adam Merrick.

Seth said it's an effect of the tropics.

Maybe he's right, Jen. I don't know. I don't feel like I'm any different, you know? Not inside. Maybe it's just when you take your same, normal self to a new place and are around new people that everyone else sees you differently. That's my theory, anyway. Or is it a hypothesis?

I know, you're thinking: typical Summer, trying to analyze everything when she should just be enjoying it. But I have to think about it, at least a little. It's like if I'm still me, why are people acting differently toward me? And if I'm *not* me, then . . . who am I?

And if I don't know who I am, how am I supposed to know how I feel about things? I tell Seth to take a hike because he's got a girlfriend already and because I'm not the kind of girl who goes out with guys who already have girlfriends. But who says I'm that kind of girl? Maybe I'm not. Or maybe in Minnesota I was, and here I'm not.

I am totally a mess. Lost and confused.

Or maybe I'm just sleepy.

13

Fishnets, Reeboks, and Lost Loves

G ood morning, Frank," Summer said.

The bird gave her a fishy look and turned away.

"Must be the uniform," Summer muttered. She was dressed in her brand-new Crab 'n' Conch uniform, consisting of a too-short, white-and-blue sailor-suit dress, a white apron with a huge starched bow, fishnet panty hose, a really dorky sailor hat, and her own black Reeboks.

"What would *Sassy* or *Seventeen* say about combining black leather running shoes and fishnets?" she asked Frank. "I'm thinking it's a major 'fashion don't.'"

Frank spread his wings and flapped off.

Pretty much the same reaction as the one she'd gotten from Diver that morning. She'd gone into the bathroom to change and had emerged as he was

117

eating a bowl of cold cereal. She'd been hoping for some sort of reassurance, but he had almost shuddered at the sight of her.

Like a guy with exactly one piece of clothing in the world was one to criticize.

Summer was too tired to care. Between the party, doing the latest installment of the video for Jennifer, and trying through bleary eyes to read at least some of the employee manual, she'd had very little sleep.

She ran into Diana on the lawn of the main house. Diana was in a fully reclined lawn chair, wearing a bathing suit showing off a disgustingly tan body, talking in a low murmur on a portable phone. She glanced up almost guiltily at Summer. "No, she's not here," Diana said into the receiver. "She went to work."

A pause while Diana listened, eyeing Summer's outfit pityingly.

"The Crab 'n' Conch, from the look of the uniform she was wearing," Diana told the telephone. "Yes, she looked very cute in the uniform." Rolled eyes.

Summer gave a little wave.

Diana returned her attention to her mother, a somewhat shrill voice in the phone, long distance from Ohio. "Sorry, what did you just say?"

"I asked if Summer likes the room."

"The room? The room. Oh, well, she decided she didn't want to stay in the room."

"What are you talking about, Diana?" Her mother was using her dangerous I-suspect-you've-been-up-to-something voice.

"You know what happened? She saw the stilt house and absolutely fell in love. *Her* words—'fell in love.' So she's staying out there."

Diana held the phone several inches away from her ear, anticipating the response.

"Little Summer is out in that pile of rotting wood?" Mallory shrieked.

"I know, I was surprised too," Diana said blandly. "Different people have different tastes, I guess."

"You *guess?* Why do I have the feeling you had something to do with this?"

Diana tried her best to sound outraged, but she hadn't been expecting the phone call and was unprepared. "Me? Why would I have anything to do with Summer being out in the stilt house?"

"I don't want to go into this over the phone, Diana. Just get your cousin moved into the house."

"I think she actually does prefer it out there," Diana said stubbornly. "She's kind of a private person."

"Uh-huh. I have a pretty good idea who the private person is behind this," Mallory said.

Diana offered no response. Giving her mother the silent treatment was often the most effective thing to do. Then Diana noticed with a shock that Summer hadn't left yet. She was still standing a discreet distance away, looking as if she wanted to talk to Diana.

Oh, man, had Summer been able to overhear? Maybe not—the gardener at the house next door

119

was running electric hedge clippers. Diana hoped she hadn't heard.

"Well, what's done is done, I guess," Mallory said in Diana's ear. "But there is one thing I absolutely insist on."

"What's that?" Diana asked guardedly.

"Get someone down to make that stilt house livable. Get her a decent bed, at least. You can move the one out of the guest room. And have someone make any other repairs. Call what's-his-name. The old man."

"Mr. Warner?" Diana suppressed a smile. Mr. Warner was Seth's grandfather. Seth worked for him during the summer. She liked Seth—it was almost impossible not to. He was a little like Summer in that way. The two of them should get together. They would represent more concentrated wholesomeness than existed anywhere else in the Keys.

"Yes," Mallory said, breaking into Diana's cynical reverie. "I want that stilt house made fit for a human being. Summer's mother would kill me if she saw where she's living."

"Okay," Diana said. "I'll call Mr. Warner right away. Bye." She pressed the disconnect button and put down the phone.

Well, the situation wasn't ideal. Ideal would have been scaring Summer all the way back to Minnesota. But at least this way she wouldn't really be a part of Diana's daily life.

"Diana?" Summer came back over and stood in front of Diana.

"Uh-huh? Don't you have to get to work?" Diana asked. "Black fishnets with running shoes?"

"That's the uniform," Summer said, blushing a little. "I have kind of a stupid question to ask you. I mean, maybe it's stupid, I don't know."

"What is it?"

"Well, I went to this party last night. You know, over at the Merrick estate?"

"So?"

"Well, it's just that you used to go out with Adam."

Diana's heart skipped several beats. What did Summer know about that? Had Adam actually told her something? "Used to," she said guardedly.

Summer dug her toe into the grass awkwardly. She stared down at the ground, looked up, smiled her big smile, then looked down at the ground again. "It's just that, what would you think if he was going out with someone else?"

"I guess I'd have to think something like 'life goes on,'" Diana said, sounding much cooler than she felt. In fact, her heart was pounding at near-panic intensity.

"So you don't mind if, like, I—"

"*You?* You and Adam?"

"I don't have to if it would upset you," Summer said quickly.

"Why should it upset me?" Diana asked. "It's all in the past." All of it. In the past.

"Cool," Summer said. Again the smile. "I'd better get going. Don't want to be late my first day of work."

"Have fun."

121

Summer trotted off across the grass, hurrying to make up for lost time.

Summer and Adam. Adam and Ross.

Diana shuddered and tried to thrust away the memory. It had all happened last summer, a year ago, a long time. And Ross had been doing a lot of drugs back then. A lot. And everyone said he'd calmed down quite a bit, had spent six months in rehab.

Nothing to worry about. Summer was a big girl. She could take care of herself.

In which case Summer would have Adam, Diana realized with a wrenching feeling that brought a grimace to her face.

And if Summer *couldn't* take care of herself?

"Not my problem," Diana told herself firmly. "I didn't even want her here."

"Hey, everybody, this is Summer Smith!" Marquez announced in a brassy yell that managed to carry over the roar of the dishwashing machine, the clash of plates, the pounding of knives on cutting boards, and a radio that was blaring salsa music. "She's a new waitress."

"Poor kid," another waitress remarked.

"She have a boyfriend?" the dishwasher yelled.

"Yeah, *me*," the smaller of the two male cooks replied, laughing.

"She doesn't date outside her species, Paulie," Marquez shot back.

"Good one, Marquez," offered a female cook with a nearly shaved head and a long tail of hair down the back. "She don't need none of what passes for males around here."

"Wait a minute, Skeet, *you* pass for male around here," the taller, cuter cook said.

The woman named Skeet Frisbeed a slice of tomato at him.

Marquez took Summer's arm. "The tall one who thinks he's funny is J.T. The stupid-looking one is Paulie, and that's Skeet."

"We may be stupid, but we have knives," J.T. said. "So you have to obey us in all things. Just pick up your food when it's hot and we won't have to hurt you."

Skeet and Paulie both laughed.

"Ignore them," Marquez said. "Cooks are all crazy."

They stepped out of the loud, boisterous, and brightly lit kitchen into the dining room, an area as big as a football field with what looked to Summer like a thousand tables.

"Okay," Marquez announced, "so you read the employee manual, right?"

"Yes, last night." Summer yawned.

"Cool, now forget everything in the manual. All that stuff is bull. Just follow me around and I'll teach you what to do."

"Thanks."

"Don't thank me," Marquez said, laughing. "You're my slave for the day, honey. Good thing, too, because I'm beat. I'm all sore, especially my legs from dancing."

Summer nodded. "Now what?"

"Well, we've done our setup work, we've introduced you to everyone. Now we stand around and wait till the customers start to show up. And while we're doing that, we gossip. Like you tell me more about Adam."

"Today I asked Diana if it was okay for me to go out with him," Summer said.

Marquez nodded. "That was a stand-up thing to do. I have this guy I was seeing for a long time. We just broke up a couple weeks ago, and I don't know if I'd want my cousin going out with him. What did Diana say?"

"She said she didn't care because it was all in the past."

Marquez nodded. "Yeah, she's right. Past is past."

"Tell me about this guy. The one you were going with?"

Marquez sighed. "He was okay, I guess. Only, he was screwed up in the head. His family is totally screwed up. I mean, like his mom is completely weird."

"Why did you break up?"

"Found out he was going out behind my back."

"With another girl?" Summer asked.

Marquez rolled her eyes. "Actually, it wasn't anyone, that I know of. It's just that he suddenly says he's not happy and wants to start seeing other girls. The jerk."

"Wait, so now you don't see this guy anymore?"

"I see him around," Marquez said with a shrug. "It's J.T., okay?"

"The cook? The tall one?"

"Yeah, that's him."

"But neither of you acted like . . ."

"Hey, we're at work, right? We have to deal with it, so we both act like it's no big deal."

Summer noticed a waitress crossing the dining room toward them, swinging her petite hips through the close-packed tables with practiced ease. Her red hair was swept back in a ponytail held in place with bright scrunchies.

Lianne.

"Hi, Marquez," Lianne said.

"Hey, Lianne. Back to the grind, huh?" Marquez said.

"Just like last summer," Lianne said. "This place hasn't changed. You have, though. You look wonderful, Marquez. I love your hair."

Marquez nodded noncommittally. "You two met at the party last night, right?"

"We didn't actually meet," Lianne said. She flashed a killer smile at Summer. "I was so excited to see Seth again, it was hard to concentrate on anything else. It's been *days*."

"Uh-huh. Well, Summer, meet Lianne, and vice versa. Lianne waited tables here last summer, like me," Marquez explained.

"Summer? I think that is the most beautiful name," Lianne said. "It must be great. Every time anyone thinks of you they're going to think of sunshine and warm breezes. And you have the looks to go with the name."

Summer was a little taken aback. Lianne seemed very sweet. "Thanks," Summer said, feeling flustered because she couldn't think of a way to return the compliment.

"I've heard of you, you know," Lianne said. "From Diana. She and I are good friends."

"Still?" Marquez said skeptically.

Lianne looked sad. "We *have* grown apart, I'm afraid. I suppose Diana has outgrown me." She made a wistful, bleak smile. For a moment Summer thought Lianne might actually cry.

"Diana has outgrown everyone," Marquez said.

Lianne put on a brave face and directed her smile at Summer. "Anyway, now I feel like I have a new friend. At least I hope we'll be friends, Summer."

"Sure," Summer blurted.

"Well, happy, happy, joy, joy," Marquez said dryly. She peered across the dining room and became more serious. "Okay, we have a party of two. We call that a deuce. Deuce, three-top, four-top, et cetera. Pour two glasses of water, Summer. Gossip time just ended."

Marquez took off and Summer started after her. But then she felt a hand on her arm, holding her back.

Lianne pitched her voice low, so no one else would hear. "Summer, since we are going to be friends, I should just warn you about one thing. It's Seth. I know he's pretending like we broke up, but we didn't. Seth has a little problem with the truth sometimes. And if you get in the middle, you're just going to get hurt, because Seth really does love me."

"I'm not in the middle of anything," Summer said stiffly.

"Good," Lianne said. She exhibited a brilliant smile that never reached her eyes. "Seth may not be perfect, but he's all I have."

14

The Mysteries of Paint

M y feet hurt." Summer was practically
limping through the town, across mostly
empty streets baked by the terrifying late-afternoon
sun.

Marquez had volunteered to take her shopping
for a few necessities that the stilt house lacked, like
towels and toilet paper and food. But first they had to
change out of their uniforms, which smelled of cocktail sauce and cigarette smoke. That meant walking
from the restaurant to Marquez's house and then to
Summer's house, all on painful feet and pavement
that was approximately the same temperature as the
surface of the sun. Marquez said she might be able to
borrow her parents' car for the rest of the trip.

"My feet hurt too," Marquez said, "but you'll
get used to it. At least it isn't hot out."

"It isn't?"

Marquez grinned. "It's only early June. Now, August . . ." She laughed an evil laugh. "August afternoons, I've seen people burst into flames."

"You have not."

"If you say so. All I'm saying is, don't wear polyester—that burns too fast. Come on, we're almost there."

"There" turned out to be a genteelly seedy three-story building just off the main drag. The bottom floor had once been a store. It still had a huge plate-glass window with a faded, old-fashioned sign painted on it.

"Ice Cream Parlor?" Summer read.

"Yeah, it used to be an ice cream parlor, back like fifty years ago. Upstairs was offices. My dad bought the building after he got settled in this country."

Marquez opened a side door that gave onto a narrow stairway. The entrance was made more narrow by the three bikes that were parked there. From up the stairs Summer could hear a TV or radio, the announcer speaking Spanish.

"My folks speak English too, but they like Spanish sometimes," Marquez explained, not exactly self-consciously, but as if she were waiting to see how Summer would react.

"So do you speak Spanish?" Summer asked.

"Sure. A little, anyway, just so I can talk with my grandma. My older brothers still speak it pretty well because some of them were older when we left Cuba. Well, here goes." Marquez opened a second door that led from the landing. "This is my room."

Summer stepped through the door and gasped. Then she laughed. Then she just stared, mouth hanging open. "This is your room?"

"Yeah. Different, huh?"

The room was huge, a vast, open space. Most of one wall was mirrored, with gleaming chrome shelves where Coke glasses and banana split dishes had once been stacked. Now the shelves held folded T-shirts and sweaters and shorts. Panties spilled out of a former hot fudge warmer. A menu on the wall showed the price of hot fudge sundaes as fifteen cents.

Down the middle of the room was the Formica-topped, chrome-trimmed bar, fronted by half a dozen stools bolted in place and upholstered with red plastic. The bar was cluttered with a boom box and a disorderly mess of CDs and cassettes and at least a dozen spray cans of paint.

But the most amazing thing about the room was the walls. They were bare brick—or had once been bare. Now they were coated an inch thick with wild graffiti, words a foot tall in places. There were strangely beautiful pictures, like murals, showing dazzling mountain scenes and rain forests and sunrises. In one corner of the room a palm tree had been painted all the way up the high wall, with fanned branches spreading out across a corner of the ceiling.

"You like my tree? Don't even have to water it," Marquez joked.

"Marquez. This. Is. The most *amazing* room I've ever seen. This is so excellent. This is so far past just being cool. This is a whole new planet of coolness."

"I'm glad you like it," Marquez said. "If you didn't like it, we couldn't be friends."

"Like it? It's a total work of art. You're an artist."

"No, it's just playing-around art. I got this room because I'm the only girl," Marquez said. "I have five brothers. My older brothers got rooms with views of the water, and my younger brothers share a room whenever my older brothers are around, which they are only sometimes." She counted off on her fingers. "Tony is in the army and he's in Germany. Miguel and Raoul are in college, only they're home for the summer now. Ronnie is going into tenth grade and he's a monster, and George is going to start eighth."

"How come everyone got Spanish names except Ronnie and George?" Summer asked. "Is it okay if I ask that?" She was still walking around, head tilted back, taking in the amazing details.

"Sure, why not? Ronnie and George were the first ones born in this country. So they got named after, guess who? *Ronald* Reagan and *George* Bush."

Summer smiled. "You guys sound so interesting. I mean, escaping from Cuba and this room and all. My family is so boring. Plus five brothers. I never had any siblings. You know, except for Jonathan, and like I said, I never knew him except from some pictures."

"Have a seat on the bed," Marquez said, nodding toward the king-size bed in front of the curtained shop window. "I just want to change out of this uniform and we can go."

Summer sat and let her eyes wander over the walls. Much of the graffiti was names. Names of TV stars and musicians, names of fictional characters from books, names that could be anyone. And what could only be called thoughts or slogans.

"'J.T.,'" Summer read out loud. "Is that the same J.T.?" The letters were about three feet tall, red and rimmed with black so they stood out as though they were three-dimensional.

"Yeah, that's him." Marquez was stripping off her uniform, showing none of the modesty Summer would have, even in front of another girl.

"I would have thought you'd paint over it."

"No, that's not the way it works. Once something goes on the wall, it never gets deliberately painted over. Maybe over time, months and months or whatever, a little gets covered here, and a little more there until it's almost all gone. But you can't just wipe out the past."

Summer grinned. "Very deep."

Marquez laughed. "You probably didn't know I was so philosophical, right?"

Summer was about to ask whether she would eventually be invited to add her name to the wall. To be added and never deliberately erased or painted over. A strange kind of immortality, like something permanent left behind when she left Crab Claw Key.

"Ready?" Marquez asked. She had slipped on a tube top and shorts. "I'm ready to shop. Our car's out front. Let me just run upstairs and see if we can take it."

*　　*　　*

Diana saw them pull into the driveway in the Marquez family's huge, aging Oldsmobile. She was upstairs assembling a pile of washcloths, towels, and sheets to carry down to the stilt house. It was a shame Summer was home so early. It would have been better to have everything done. Diana was prepared to comply with her mother's orders to make the stilt house comfortable. She just didn't want to be seen acting generous.

Summer was wearing her absurd uniform. Marquez was dressed like a slut, as usual. As they got out of the car they both started giggling, sharing some joke.

Diana felt a stab of jealousy. At this moment Summer was already more a part of life on Crab Claw Key than Diana, though Diana had lived here most of her life. Summer had a job, a friend—probably a boyfriend, soon, if Adam really was interested in her.

Diana remembered when her own life had been more that way. When there had been friends, boyfriends, reasons to start giggling over nothing.

Diana headed down the stairs and caught up with them as they were heading down the lawn toward the stilt house.

"Hey, Summer," Diana said.

Summer and Marquez turned.

"Hey, *Di-Anne,*" Marquez said.

"Hello, *Maria,*" Diana answered. She hated when people mispronounced her name. Almost as much as Marquez hated being called Maria. "So nice to see you again. I was so afraid that now that I've graduated, I wouldn't see you anymore. Terrified, in fact."

"I've been thinking about you, Di-*anne*. See, I heard this guy was found dead over on the new side, right? And there were these two little holes in his neck, and all the blood had been drained out of him, so naturally, I thought of you right away."

"Amusing as always, Maria. Those paint fumes in your room blurring your vision again? Or is there some other reason for the way you're dressed?" Diana turned quickly to Summer before Marquez could come up with a reply. "I just wanted to tell you, before you go down to the stilt house, that someone's there."

Summer's response was surprising. Her face went blank and her eyes grew wide. "No, there isn't," she said quickly.

"Yes, there is," Diana said.

Summer shook her head almost violently. "There's no one there that I know about, and I would know, right? If you found something there that looked like there was someone there, then maybe it was something of mine and just looked like somebody else's."

Diana looked at Marquez. "Did you understand that?"

Marquez shook her head, equally puzzled.

"Summer, let me try this more slowly this time." Diana sighed. "Seth Warner is down at the stilt house. He's doing some work on it, fixing it up."

"*Seth!* Oh, Seth," Summer said, looking inexplicably relieved. "Seth. Okay, Seth is down there. Not anyone else though, right?"

"Who were you expecting?" Diana asked sourly. "Adam?"

"No, I'm not supposed to be seeing him till tomorrow night."

Summer and Marquez started again for the stilt house and Diana fell in step behind them, still carrying her gift of towels.

Summer found the house looking strange. Water was dripping from the eaves and from the railing and was puddling on the deck, though it hadn't been raining. Plus, something was missing.

"The bird crap!" Summer said. "It's gone." The pelican was sitting on his usual corner but was looking disgruntled. "Frank, you okay?"

"*Frank?*" Diana asked.

"Um, well, that's what I call him," Summer said quickly. "You know, just a name I made up."

Summer stepped over a toolbox and paint-splattered canvas drop cloth.

From inside the house there was the sound of a radio or stereo playing. The Breeders. And a male voice was singing along, changing the lyrics. "I'm just looking for the div-i-ne paintbrush. One div-i-ne paintbrush. I'd brush it all day . . ."

Instantly, as if on command, the three girls froze and fell silent. Marquez raised one eyebrow, playfully suggestive. She quietly opened the tool-box and extracted a hammer.

Stifling giggles, they tiptoed to the door.

"One divine paintbrush, one div-i-ine paint-brush . . ."

Diana opened the door. Seth was standing on a short ladder, his bare shoulders splattered with little drops of white paint, wearing shorts and work boots. He was using a roller to apply paint to the ceiling.

"We couldn't find the divine paintbrush," Diana said.

"But we have the divine hammer," Marquez said, holding it up.

"That was just the DJ singing along," Seth said lamely.

"Oh. I believe that," Marquez said. "Don't you believe that, Diana? Even though it's a CD, not the radio."

"I didn't know Mr. Moon could sing," Diana said. "I knew he had other attributes, but I didn't know he could sing."

Seth climbed down off the ladder and rested his roller in the paint pan. "Okay, I'll ask you again, Diana, what will it take to get that picture from you? And the negative, too."

Summer noticed the paint splats on his skin. Some had dried already, and the effect was to make the skin itself look soft and warm.

"I thought I'd give that picture to Summer," Diana said. "She could hang it on these nice white walls."

Summer blushed as badly as Seth did.

"The two of you, you're both so sweet," Marquez said. "Look at them blush."

"So is white paint okay? It's off-white, actually," Seth said to Summer, clearly trying to change the subject.

"It looks great," Summer said coolly. There had to be other people who could do this work. So why was Seth there?

"I did the walls earlier, so they're almost dry. Then I hosed off the outside, and I figured I might as well start on the ceiling. And there's the bed," Seth said, pointing, as if a new double bed could somehow be invisible in the small room. He seemed to be trying very hard to act professional. "You want to get rid of the old one?"

Summer looked inquiringly at Diana. Had this repair and cleanup work been Diana's idea?

Diana shrugged. "I thought since you *insisted* on staying down here instead of staying in the main house that at least we could fix things up a little. So I called Mallory and asked her if I could have the place fixed up for you."

"That was awfully nice of you," Summer said dubiously. She wasn't normally a skeptical person, but Diana's story sounded slightly unlikely. That morning it had sounded as if Aunt Mallory was yelling at Diana on the phone.

Seth laughed. "Yeah, and then Diana's mom called my grandfather long distance and said we should do the work regardless of what Diana said or did to stop us."

"Must be the paint fumes, Seth," Diana said without much sincerity. "You obviously misunderstood."

"You're getting a new paint job, bird crap removal, and some new flooring in the bathroom and the kitchen," Seth told Summer. "You can come with me and pick out the tile after I get cleaned up. If you'd like. You don't have to, but you could have your choice, and there's lots of kinds of tile. Also we're going to run cable down from the house." He put a finger to his lips. "Only don't tell anyone about that, because it isn't exactly legal."

From outside came the sound of a boat motor, loud at first, then gentling to an idle. A horn sounded.

"Anyone home?" a voice called.

"That sounds like Adam," Summer said. Her heart began beating very fast.

Again she felt an inexplicable sense of guilt. As though there was something wrong in letting Seth know she was seeing Adam. Or the reverse.

"*Is* that Adam's voice?" Marquez asked Diana, batting her eyes provocatively.

Diana said nothing. Summer opened the door and went outside. A large motorboat had nosed under the house. Behind it trailed the two Jet Skis, bobbing on the wake.

"Adam?" Summer called, but he was concealed from view beneath the house. She went back inside as the floor hatch opened and Adam climbed up, smiling his seductive, mocking, maximum-power smile until his eyes fell on Diana. Something dark and unfathomable passed between Adam and Diana.

"Hi," Adam said, in a general sort of way. Then, "Hi, Summer."

Summer saw his eyes dart to Diana again and then away. Diana crossed her arms coolly. No matter what Diana said, there was something powerful between the two of them. Some potent, disturbing emotion that Summer couldn't read.

"I was going to ask what had happened to the Jet Skis," Diana said. "I noticed they were gone."

"They left them at my place," Adam said curtly. "Seth, my man, what's up?"

"Just doing some work. You've heard of work, right?"

The two guys were eyeing each other warily, Summer noticed, but without hostility.

"I may have heard something about it," Adam said, smiling good-naturedly at the sort of teasing he'd obviously heard many times before. "Work. Yes, I think one of the servants may have mentioned it once. Speaking of which, want to give me a hand getting those skis tied off?"

Seth headed below with Adam.

Marquez shook her head. "You are something, Summer," she said.

"What? What do you mean?"

"You just breeze into town and already you've got two A-list guys interested in you," Marquez said. "Not that either of them is my type, so what do I care."

"No, your type would be more the slightly

deranged, mentally unstable type, *Maria*," Diana said with surprising intensity.

"I don't think either of them is interested in me," Summer protested weakly. "I *know* Seth isn't," she lied. "He has a girlfriend. Maybe Adam . . . Oh, you guys are just teasing me."

"Are you blind?" Marquez demanded in a loud whisper. "Of course Seth is interested in you. Didn't you see that little guy thing between him and Adam?"

"You're crazy," Summer said, a little too forcefully.

"Seth is a nice guy," Diana said, almost to herself. She chewed a fingernail.

Marquez sent Summer a significant look. "Oh, *Seth* is a nice guy, huh? As opposed to Adam? Hmmmm."

Diana narrowed her eyes and seemed to snap back to the present. "Shut up, *Maria*. It's totally over between me and Adam. Just because you can't get over J.T. doesn't mean I have the same problem."

"I repeat—hmmmm."

The hatch in the floor opened, and Adam emerged, followed by Seth. For a moment they formed a single picture, framed against the dark opening. Seth thinner, perhaps a little taller. Adam darker, more muscular. It was amazing to think that they *were* interested in her, Summer thought. Amazing and disturbing in a way, like maybe it was all some elaborate practical joke.

"So what are you girls up to?" Adam asked.

Marquez answered. "Summer and I were going

to do some shopping in town, or else drive down to Key West and hit some stores there."

"Cool," Adam said. "Why don't I give you a lift down to Key West in the boat? It's as fast as driving there, and no traffic."

"Um, look, um, Summer," Seth began, "if you want to look at some tiles, you know . . ." He let the question peter out and made a wry face. "Let's see. Go to the hardware store to look at tiles or boat down to Key West. Wow, tough choice."

"Actually," Summer said, a little too quickly, "Marquez and I are going shopping for girl-type stuff, so it should probably be just a girl trip."

"Yeah, besides, guys don't know how to shop," Marquez said, picking up on Summer's hint.

"Diana, would you come with us?" Summer asked.

"What are you shopping for?" Adam asked suspiciously. "I know how to shop just fine."

"Let's see," Marquez said, "what was on our list?" She began counting off on her fingers. "Oh, yeah, makeup and shampoo, and of course panty shields and lots of tampons."

"Oh. You know, we could look at tiles another day," Seth said quickly.

"The thing is, I just remembered I have to get home," Adam said just as quickly. "But I'll pick you up tomorrow evening, Summer, okay?"

"And I'll be by to finish the painting tomorrow," Seth said.

"I can drop you at the dock," Adam offered to Seth.

"Cool. Later, everyone."

"That worked pretty well," Diana said when the two guys had escaped down through the hatch. "Nothing like the word *tampon* for clearing guys away. What are you two really shopping for?"

"Whatever," Marquez said.

"Come with us, Diana," Summer said again.

"I don't think so," Diana said.

"Doesn't want to be seen with the riffraff," Marquez muttered.

Summer took Diana's hand. Something made Summer feel Diana wanted to go with them. "Come on. You have to come."

"Well, if I have to," Diana said testily. "If I *have* to, I guess I will."

15

Purchases

SUMMER
(using the spending money her parents gave her)

Buf Puf̃s
Sea Breeze
Hawaiian Tropic SPF 8–10
Dove soap
Generic disposable razors (5 pack)
Bare Assets two-piece bathing suit
Pepperidge Farm raisin bread
Skippy Extra Chunky
Oreos
Milk 1% fat
2 Dannon Yogurt (blueberry and raspberry)
Ben & Jerry's Cherry Garcia frozen yogurt
Jiffy Pop
Advil

Breeders CD
July issue of *Seventeen*
TOTAL: $90.14

MARQUEZ
(using the tip money from the lunch shift)

Express Ltd. white denim shorts (on sale)
Snickers bar
TOTAL: $19.55

DIANA
(using her mother's Visa Gold Card)

Lancôme Bienfait Total
Jean Paul Gaultier bra top and sarong skirt
Abe Hamilton linen gauze dress
Crest Fresh Mint Gel
July issue of *Sassy*
TOTAL: $532.35

16

Summer's Heinous Truths and Diana's Little Pills

Your calves are not chunky, for heaven's sake," Marquez said, throwing her hands up in exasperation. "Your little Minnesota calves are perfect. You have the calves of Elle MacPherson. And she's probably wanting them back."

Summer turned sideways to check the effect of her new bathing suit in Diana's full-length mirror. For the twentieth time. "But it does make my butt look huge."

"Your butt wouldn't look huge if you stuffed a pair of beach balls back there," Marquez said, thoroughly disgusted. She slapped her own rear end, barely contained within the very short shorts she'd bought. "Now, *this* is a big butt."

Diana emerged from the bathroom, wearing the white gauze dress she'd bought for more than the cost of Summer's entire wardrobe. She stood thoughtfully in front of the mirror and looked at herself critically.

"Don't *you* even start," Marquez warned.

"It looks okay," Diana allowed.

"For what it cost it should look okay," Marquez said.

Diana nodded. "We used to not have any money back when I was in junior high. Before Mallory started writing her trashy books, back when it was just my dad trying to support us. So, I've done the life-on-a-budget thing." She made a wry smile. "Lose a father, gain really good clothes."

"Is that why your parents broke up?" Summer asked.

"Who knows," Diana said. "That's what most of the arguments were about. That and sex."

Summer winced. "They talked about that in front of you?"

"No. They just talked in very loud voices so that even people who lived in the next block got to hear."

"Gross," Summer said, making a face.

Marquez flopped back on Diana's bed. She rummaged in the Oreos Summer had bought and twisted one open. "Truth or dare?" she said suddenly.

"Forget it," Diana said flatly. "If you two start that junior high stuff, I'll kick you both out."

"I can't believe you haven't kicked us out already, Diana," Marquez said. "Is this like reverse PMS or something? Your hormones are making you be nice?"

"Don't put your shoes on the bedspread, *Maria*."

Marquez grinned, threw back the covers, and stuck her shoes under the sheet. "This better?"

"Are you *trying* to annoy me?"

"Come on, you guys," Summer said, "don't fight." It was a phrase she'd had to use at least half a dozen times during their shopping excursion. And though Diana and Marquez had sniped at each other in one store and out another, Diana had seemed happier than she had since Summer had arrived in Florida. She'd been almost giddy at times.

But since they'd returned home, Diana's mood seemed to have grown darker. It was as if she was making up for the fact that she'd had a good time.

"Okay, truth or dare," Diana said suddenly, her eyes lighting up. "For you, Summer."

Summer sat down on Diana's desk chair and put her hands on her knees. "Truth, I guess. But throw me an Oreo first, Marquez." She hoped Diana wasn't going to ask her about Adam.

"Good. Here's the question, and I want the truth." Diana was fixing on her with way too much intensity. "Why did you come down here?"

Summer sighed with relief. "Because it sounded cool. I mean, the beach and everything."

"Yeah, yeah, but why, really?" Diana pressed. She was standing over Summer, looking simultaneously imperious and very much like an angel in her gauzy dress.

"That's it. When your mom called my mom I was having this terrible day. I was freezing—which is pretty much every day in the winter in

147

Minnesota—and my friend Jennifer was going away to California for the summer, and this guy, this jerk named Sean Valletti who I thought I had a crush on, had started going out with this other girl just because she has massive . . . Never mind."

"What did Mallory tell you?" Diana pressed. "Didn't she tell you that I was being a pain or something?"

Marquez jumped in. "Why would she have to tell Summer that? Everyone who knows you knows you're a pain, Diana."

"Diana, what are you saying?" Summer asked. "You think this was some kind of a conspiracy or something?" Summer would have laughed, only Diana looked so serious.

"I *know* what Mallory was thinking. I'm just wondering if she told you."

Summer shook her head solemnly. "No one told me anything. Why? Is something the matter?"

Diana looked nonplussed. She shook her head distractedly. "Oh, my mom, I mean, Mallory, thinks I'm depressed or using drugs or something. She wanted you to come down and cheer me up, because she can't be bothered to worry about me herself."

"*Are* you depressed?" Summer asked.

"Of course not," Diana said quickly. Her words gathered momentum. "Why would I be depressed? I'm *not* depressed. Besides, it's none of your business, Summer. Believe it or not, we all had lives going on here even before you showed up."

There was a shocked silence.

Diana took a deep breath. "Sorry. I have this headache."

Summer shook her head and sent Marquez a sad look. She held out an Oreo for Diana. "Here, don't be depressed."

"I'm not depressed," Diana snapped. "It's not like I'm lying awake at night thinking about ways to kill myself."

For several seconds her statement hung in the air between them, and no one spoke. They had all three heard something false, something ragged and raw in Diana's voice.

"Okay, my turn," Marquez said, breaking the silence. "Also for you, Summer. Truth or dare?"

"Truth. I don't trust you with a dare." The moment was past. Maybe it had never even occurred. How could she hope to read Diana's thoughts? Summer asked herself. She barely knew her cousin.

"You're a smart girl," Marquez told Summer. "Never trust me with a dare. Here's the question. Are you really as sweet as you seem or is there some dark, twisted inner core of hostility inside you?"

Summer laughed. "Definitely dark and twisted."

"Oh, there is not," Marquez said. "If you were really dark and twisted, like a certain person in this room who shall remain nameless but whose name rhymes with banana, you'd never admit it."

Diana managed a wistful smile. "That's right."

"I'm not totally sweet," Summer said defensively.

"Sure. Right." Marquez grinned expectantly.

"I'm *not*." Summer was beginning to get annoyed. *Sweet* was something she'd left behind in Bloomington.

"Okay, then prove it. What's the sleaziest, most heinous thing you've ever done?"

Summer thought frantically. Marquez and Diana were both eyeing her doubtfully, waiting for her to admit that she couldn't think of anything. "Do dreams count? Because I have great dreams. And I usually remember them."

"No way," Marquez said. "If dreams counted, I'd be arrested."

"How about this?" Summer said with sudden defiance. "I kissed a total stranger once." She saw Marquez dart a glance at Diana. Oh, no, Marquez was thinking of Adam! "Actually, it happened twice," Summer said quickly, "and the first time was the most heinous." She hoped Marquez would get the message.

She did. "Drunk or sober?" Marquez asked.

"Sober. So I had no excuse. I just let him kiss me. It was in a photo booth."

Marquez shrugged. "That's not heinous, Summer. It sounds like fun."

"It was heinous enough," Summer said. But clearly neither girl was impressed. "Okay, fine. Try this. I let a guy spend the night with me."

Marquez and Diana both snapped to attention.

"I mean, we didn't do *it* or anything. It wasn't like that," Summer said quickly.

Both Marquez and Diana relaxed.

"Actually, he kind of spent the night outside my room." On the deck over her roof, to be exact, and nothing whatsoever had happened between them. He wasn't even interested, because it would disturb his *wa*, whatever that meant. But there was no reason to tell that to these two.

"So, some guy slept outside your room in Minnesota? Hope it wasn't winter," Diana said.

"No, it was summer," Summer said evasively. She wasn't ready to tell anyone about Diver. Or Seth.

But she couldn't help wondering that the only remotely heinous events she could think of happened during the few days she'd been in Florida.

Marquez sighed and shook her head in disappointment. "Well, that was pretty heinous, Summer. I'm horrified. Aren't you horrified, Diana? Call 911."

"It was the most terrible thing I've ever heard," Diana said. "I don't know how I'll ever be able to sleep tonight."

Summer stewed resentfully. Maybe if she could have told them all the details, that the first guy had a girlfriend already. Ha! Or that the second guy was totally awesomely cute. That he never wore any real clothes. That he appeared in her bedroom while she was asleep. That he talked to pelicans . . . no, that wouldn't help.

"Fine, now it's *my* turn," Summer said. "For you, Marquez. Truth or dare?"

"Dare."

"No, say truth, I don't have a dare," Summer said.

"Okay, truth."

"I want to know two things. Why did you break up with J.T. and were you doing it with him?" Ha, that would show Marquez. Maybe she wasn't heinous, but she could ask heinous questions.

"It?" Marquez repeated with a slow drawl. "What can you possibly mean by *it?*"

"Just answer the question."

Marquez put her hand over her heart. "I am still a virgin, if that's what you mean." She batted her eyes. "Why did I break up with J.T.? Because he's crazy, I told you."

"Crazy is kind of vague," Diana offered.

Marquez shrugged. "Okay. Okay. Fine." She stood up, evidently enjoying being the center of attention. "See, he got cut pretty bad at work, right? This is like three weeks ago, right? Maybe a month. Some of the cooks were screwing around throwing knives like idiots, which is what cooks are. So he's gushing out blood from his neck and they rush him to the hospital and they're saying he may need a blood transfusion, right? He didn't, but that doesn't matter."

"It doesn't?" Summer asked.

Marquez waved her off impatiently. "No, it doesn't matter. Anyway, his mom is there by this time. So they're going to use her blood if it's compatible. Only it isn't. And his dad gets there, and they check him, and *his* blood isn't right, either."

"So?" Summer asked.

"So? So it turns out J.T.'s parents aren't his parents. He's adopted. He finds this out while he's lying there bleeding." Marquez shook her head sadly. She was no longer pretending to enjoy the story. Her voice grew softer, till it was hard to hear her. "I guess he couldn't handle it. After that he started getting weirder. At first I thought it was because he got cut so bad. I mean, he said while he was unconscious he was having all these visions and things. Anyway, he got distant and wouldn't talk about anything. Then he tells me out of the blue that he wants to see other girls." Marquez flopped back onto the bed.

Summer was sorry she'd asked. Marquez was so down now, and she'd been so happy. "This is a stupid game," she said.

Marquez made a noise deep in her throat and wiped at a tear. "Don't worry, Summer. It isn't your fault."

Diana looked almost as depressed as Marquez. And the mood was hard to shake off.

"Great. Now we're all feeling lousy," Marquez said. "There's only one way to get over this. Diana, we need some entertainment."

"What?" Summer asked, ready for any help.

"Ah, yes, Maria," Diana said. "I'll get my photo album."

"I don't know, Diana," Marquez said. "Summer may be too sweet."

"I am *not* sweet," Summer said. "Besides, what does looking at pictures have to do with being too sweet? Pictures are . . . Oh. *That* picture."

★   ★   ★

After they had gone, Diana lay in her bed, holding the photo. Not the infamous one of poor Seth, but the picture she had taken of Adam. In it he was just waking up, looking confused, with his hair tousled, one eye closed. In the photo, taken aboard his father's yacht, he looked vulnerable, something he never looked the rest of the time. He'd been waterskiing earlier in the day, and the sun and exercise had made him sleepy. Diana had gone below and spent an hour just watching him sleep, while up on deck the usual loud Merrick family party was under way.

She remembered the moment perfectly, every detail. How she had silently wound her camera and taken shot after shot of Adam sleeping, curled in a ball on the narrow bunk. She had kissed him ever so gently on the lips, and, as he had awakened, taken the last shot on the roll.

That had been two days before the last day with Adam.

She had developed the film a week after. She had taken scissors and cut each of the other pictures into tiny pieces and burned the pieces in a trash can, causing an awful, oily smoke.

She had saved this one picture. She hadn't been able to destroy it.

Summer had seen the picture an hour before, and Diana had easily read the look in her eyes, the interest. Summer had looked guilty, realizing somehow that this picture meant something to Diana.

Was that why Diana had shown it to her? Was that why Diana had spent the afternoon shopping with Summer, and hanging out with Summer? So that she could find a way to let Summer know how she still felt about Adam?

Diana put the picture back and hugged the album to her chest.

She had tried to bury those feelings. She had wanted to forget the sick mixture of love and contempt, desire and betrayal. But Adam had gone after Summer and stirred the feelings up again.

Diana got up, set the album aside, and walked down the hall, down the curving staircase to her mother's wing of the house. Through the ludicrous *Gone With the Wind* bedroom with its canopied bed and frills. To the vast bathroom, with the oversize marble tub raised on a platform and surrounded by lush plants. Mallory had had herself photographed there in the tub, just her head and shoulders visible through discreet clouds of bubble bath. Printed in *Romantic Times* magazine, the photo was supposedly a portrait of the romance author dreaming up her newest hero.

Diana opened the medicine cabinet. The bottle was still there, on the middle shelf. Twenty-three pills. She spilled them into her palm and counted them again. Yes, twenty-three. More than enough.

She could do it tonight. The maid would find her in the morning. Her mother would have to rush home from her tour.

Where? At the bottom of the stairs, perhaps, dramatically sprawled there? On her mother's bed? And the note—should she leave a note? A note telling the world what had happened that night, one year ago, at the estate of the famous and wealthy Merrick clan?

Not tonight, Diana decided. She was due to go to the center tomorrow. Lanessa would be expecting her. Lanessa, the helpless little girl who couldn't even speak of what had been done to her.

Diana put the pills carefully back in the bottle, returned the bottle to the shelf, and closed the mirrored door.

17

Bubble Baths and Dreams of Sunrise

Summer was in the bathtub, lying with her head back, eyes closed, and a magazine hanging from one limp hand, when she heard the knock at the door. Her first thought was that it must be Diver. But Diver didn't knock. Diver just appeared.

Her second thought was that she wasn't going to answer it. It had been a long, tiring, emotional day. The hot water felt good. The white mountain of bubbles smelled like vanilla and melon.

Again the knock came, loud but not aggressive.

Summer sighed, which sent a little flurry of bubbles flying. "I'm coming!" she yelled grumpily.

She climbed out, wrapped her terry-cloth robe around her, and padded on wrinkled bare feet to the door. "Who is it?"

"It's Seth."

Summer's breath caught in her throat. She

clutched the robe securely, cursing the fact that she'd lost the belt.

She opened the door. Seth was standing close, almost as if he'd had his nose pressed against the door. Summer was surprised by his nearness and clumsily backed away, waving her hand in a vague invitation to come inside.

Seth stepped past her. He looked at her, taking in the robe and the wet strands of her hair, and winced. "Oh, sorry. You were taking a shower, I guess."

"A bath, actually," Summer said.

"Be careful in there, by the way. The floor isn't in great shape."

"Is that what you came by to tell me?" Summer wasn't in the mood to be hospitable. She felt at a disadvantage, wearing only a robe.

"I was hoping I could, you know . . . talk to you. About . . . stuff." He swallowed hard, clearly unsure of what to say. "Is it okay if I sit down?"

"Seth, I'm kind of in the middle of taking a bath, and I'm tired, you know?"

Suddenly, as if he were being propelled by some outside force, Seth came toward her. He put his hands on her upper arms and drew her close.

"No!" Summer pushed him away with a hand on his chest.

Seth looked stricken. "I just wanted to . . . I thought . . . everything was so perfect the other day, in the airport."

"What do you think you're doing?" Summer demanded.

"I just thought if we kissed again, that everything would be fine."

Summer almost laughed. "That's what you thought? Um, excuse me, but it isn't that easy."

He ran a hand through his hair. "I guess not. I guess not. Look, the thing is, I keep thinking about you. And today when you came back and I was here, it was the same feeling, like I couldn't forget you. Like you were all I could think about."

"Seth, we don't even know each other. All we did was kiss once."

"We talked at the party," he said.

"You told me I was losing control. That wasn't exactly talking. And, oh, by the way, the conversation ended when Lianne showed up."

"I couldn't help that," Seth said.

"It didn't look to me like you were trying to help that."

"What was I supposed to do? Shove her away and make a big scene in front of everyone? We may be broken up, but we were together for a long time and I'm not going to be mean suddenly. I don't *hate* her."

"Look, forget it. This is silly, this whole thing. We kissed, so what? You don't even know me."

He started to say something, then stopped himself. "Okay, maybe you're right. That doesn't change how I feel about you, though. Ever since that day in the airport . . . It's like, like something I can't explain, Summer. But there's just this feeling in my head that you're the one."

"What one?"

He shrugged and looked miserable. "I don't know. Fate or something. Like you and I belong together."

Summer swallowed hard. "Did you use this same line on Lianne?"

"No," he said. "I never felt this way about her."

"Yeah, right," Summer said weakly.

Silence fell between them.

"Sorry. I'm putting too much pressure on you, aren't I?"

"A little," Summer said. "I mean, look, you seem very nice, and we had this one kiss—"

"Two kisses," he interrupted.

"Even if it was ten, that doesn't mean we're anything special to each other," Summer said.

"So if that doesn't mean anything," Seth asked, "what does?"

"I don't know," Summer said softly. She felt worn out. Dead beat. She had the feeling she was winning an argument she didn't really want to win.

Again silence fell.

"All I want is a chance. I see you going with Adam and think I'll never even get a chance. And this is important to me." He hesitated again, then forged ahead in a flurry of words. "I know you think I'm nuts or just feeding you some line, but this feeling I have is so incredibly powerful and so real . . . I can't believe you don't feel it too. I can't believe the . . . that the walls aren't vibrating with it, that the . . . that the air around us doesn't just catch fire."

The air may not have caught fire, but a prickly blush began to crawl up Summer's neck. For a mo-

ment she *did* feel it—a feeling like gravity, like mag-
netism, a strange craving drawing her to him. The
distance between them seemed to warp and shrink.

Summer made a noise like a whimper. It was a
whimper, but she tried to disguise it with a cough.

"Summer, all I want is a chance. I'm not saying
don't go out with Adam. I'd like to be able to say
that," he added with a rueful half-smile, "but I know
I don't have the right. Just don't shut me out, okay?"

"What does that mean?" Summer asked.

"It means give me a chance. You said we don't
know each other, so let me get to know you better."

"Uh-huh, okay," Summer said. This at least was
safer ground.

"Okay? Really?" he said. He looked awfully
sweet when he smiled that way. "Look, we'll do
something that isn't like a real date, okay?"

Summer almost laughed. "Maybe we could go
pick out some tile together."

"Perfect! When?"

"I have to work tomorrow, and I told Marquez
I'd hit the beach with her for a while. How about
tomorrow evening? I'm free till around eight."

"Excellent. Excellent. What happens at eight?
Oh. Adam, huh?" He digested the import of that.
"That's okay. Come to my house, all right? My
house is nearer the beach."

"Your house, after the beach. Now can I go
back to my bath?"

"Sure. Only step light around that part of the
floor where the linoleum is all cracked, okay?"

Summer put her hand over her heart. "I promise."

He seemed unable to stop grinning. "I'll just leave, then."

"Good night."

He started toward the door, practically dancing over to it.

"Just one thing," Summer said. "You're telling me the truth about you and Lianne, aren't you? It's really, really important." He held up three fingers close together. "Scout's honor."

She laughed. "You weren't really a Boy Scout?"

"Absolutely."

Summer heard him whistling as he walked away down the planks of the pier.

Summer fell asleep early. She was unbelievably tired. Tired of laughing and arguing with Marquez and Diana. Tired of turning Seth and Adam and Diver over and over in her mind. It had been a very, very long day, full of new experiences.

The room still reeked a little of paint fumes from the work Seth had done earlier. She'd opened all the windows, but the smell was still there, trapped in the house.

She lay there in the dark, on the new, soft bed with pillows that smelled of fabric softener, not mildew, and listened to the water slapping the pilings outside.

Sometime in the night, rain began to fall loudly on the roof, dripping from the eaves outside the window.

Summer woke when hands reached under her sheet and gently lifted her up. There were lots of hands, and as she looked around her she saw Diver and Seth and Adam. They were raising her from the bed and carrying her between them as if she were paralyzed and they were taking her to the hospital, or perhaps like she was a sacrifice and they were carrying her to the altar.

Each of them had a tarot card hanging on a string around his neck. Summer focused and she could see the cards, but for some reason couldn't connect them to the faces. At a distance stood a fourth guy, face in shadow, laughing and dressed all in white.

Summer wasn't scared, not quite. She felt giddy and sick, like she might throw up. They held her by her arms and legs, and one held her head supported in his hands and bent low to her—for a kiss? No, because they had carried her right back to her bed and now could no longer be seen.

Instead there was Marquez, her body painted in serpentine scrawls of color, dancing all alone.

And in her bed Summer was being drawn by the music, disturbing music that was all shifting tunes and melodies that never seemed to coalesce.

Then the room was silent and Diana was there, a faraway figure dressed like an angel. Summer got out of her bed and tried to go to her, but Diana kept receding, growing smaller and farther away.

A face, very near her own. Adam? Seth? A little of both. And Diver.

A kiss, the most fleeting contact, not on her lips, but on her forehead. Something wet.

Diver, barely visible in moonlight, at the side of her bed, holding the framed photograph of Summer's parents. Looking thoughtfully at them, sad, it seemed to Summer, faraway and sad.

At some point, Summer realized, she had slipped over the line to consciousness, but when exactly she couldn't say.

She only knew that the sounds she heard now were the sounds of reality. The drip of water from the eaves. The sound of her own breathing.

"Hi," she said.

"Oh," Diver said. "I didn't mean to wake you up." He replaced the framed photograph on the stand beside Summer's bed. "It's raining, so I came in."

"Good," Summer said.

"New bed, huh?"

"They left the old one. Anytime you want to use it . . ."

He shook his head. "Only when it's raining."

"I know. I would disturb your *wa*, right?"

He smiled.

"This is the second time I've gotten up from a dream and seen you. Sometimes I'm not sure you're real. Maybe you're part of a dream," she said softly.

He shrugged. "Could be."

"What time is it?" Summer asked.

"The sun is just ready to come up."

"I've been having some very strange dreams."

"This place is full of paint fumes. They're not

good for you, you know. You should come outside, get some oxygen. That will clear out your brain."

Summer nestled down under her sheet. "Too sleepy."

He reached out a hand, and without thinking, she took it. She had never touched him before. He felt real.

"Come on," he said. "You're polluted."

He pulled her from the bed and drew her to the door. Outside the world was gray, with shapes barely distinct. Frank refolded a wing and snuggled his neck back against his feathers. The air was almost cool and very wet. Summer's baby-tee clung to her clammily.

Diver ascended the ladder that ran up the side of the house to the flat part of the roof, just over her own bedroom.

"Is this where you sleep?" she asked, when she had joined him.

He nodded. "Here, sit. This way, toward the east."

Summer obeyed and folded up her knees, wrapping her arms around them. The baby-tee and boxers were thin and insubstantial, but the warmth of her bed still clung to her.

A faint, reddish glow could be seen on the horizon. The stars were retreating into the west. The water of the bay, so vividly green in the daylight, was black still. Here and there a light blinked from the homes across the bay. One of those lights was in the Merrick estate. Perhaps Adam, awake in his room.

Adam in his room, in a huge mansion. Seth,

somewhere to the north, in his grandfather's modest house. And Diver, so close beside her.

Images from the dream surfaced in Summer's consciousness. Unsettling images that carried unfamiliar emotions in their wake.

Summer shifted uneasily. "My *wa* is disturbed, and I don't even know what it is," she said.

"Just watch," Diver said. "Soon."

"Do you have a name? A *real* name?"

Diver put a finger to his lips. "Here he comes."

The horizon had grown rapidly brighter, violet and red and yellow. Scattered clouds were etched in orange. Then . . .

"Oh!" Summer pressed her hand over her heart. It had been so sudden. A brilliant, blinding arc of fire peeking over the edge of the world.

Diver smiled.

Down below on the railing, Frank turned his head, facing the rising sun.

And now the sky overhead seemed to ignite, to burst into flames, an impossible, overwhelming display. Colors beyond description. Colors that memory could never recall. The sky was everywhere. The sky had become the entire universe. And the two of them were the smallest, least significant specks, floating upward toward magnificence.

Summer realized that tears were coursing down her face.

Diver was looking at her, watching the tears. He nodded. "Frank was right about you. He said you were all right."

18

Diana Lies, Summer Cries, and Marquez Takes No Crap from Guys.

Diana spotted Summer on the road to town, walking along in her work uniform as though she didn't have a care in the world. Diana considered just driving on past, but as much as it made her uncomfortable to admit it, Summer had crossed a line of some sort yesterday.

You couldn't just drive by and ignore someone you'd shopped with, could you?

Diana pulled the Neon to a stop beside Summer. "Hey. Want a ride into town?"

"Sure." Summer climbed in, careful not to crush her apron bow. She had a copy of the menu on her lap.

"Off to work, huh?"

"Yes. I think they're going to let me have some tables on my own today."

"Please don't tell me that excites you," Diana said.

"I have to make some money this summer," Summer said. "I wish I didn't, but I guess it will be good experience. When I go to college I'll probably have to earn all of my spending money, even if I get a scholarship. I don't know what I'll do if I don't get a scholarship. Have you ever had a job?"

Diana shook her head. "Nope. Haven't needed one, I guess."

"Must be nice," Summer said. "You'll be able just to concentrate on classes when you go to college."

"I don't think I'm going," Diana said.

"Oh."

"It's not my grades or anything," Diana said, detecting what she thought was pity in Summer's eyes. "I got accepted all over the place. Mallory forced me to apply. But she can't force me to go."

"I have to go. I mean, if I want to get a job."

Diana smiled condescendingly. "What are you going to be when you grow up?"

"I don't know. Lately I've been thinking I could be a TV reporter. Only, I don't really enjoy having to be rude and ask people lots of questions. Where are you going?"

"I thought you didn't like asking questions. I'm just going shopping."

"I would have figured you were all shopped out after yesterday," Summer said.

"Here we are," Diana said, sidestepping the question. The institute was her own private place, not for anyone else to know about. Even her mother had no idea. She idled the car in front of the restaurant.

Summer climbed out. She hesitated, as if about to ask Diana something, then decided against it.

The manager gave Summer three tables. The first party went fine, with Marquez looking over her shoulder like a protective big sister. Then the place went wild. People seemed to be coming from everywhere, filling every table and standing ten deep at the hostess stand.

"One more piece of restaurant language you need to know," Marquez said as she bustled past Summer, carrying a huge tray load of food.

"What?" Summer asked anxiously. She was trying desperately to make sense of the insanely beeping computer precheck machine.

"In the weeds," Marquez said over her shoulder.

"What's that?"

"That's what we're in right now," Marquez said. "We are deep in the weeds."

Fill waters. Fill bread basket. Carry away dirty dishes. Check kitchen for order. Punch in drink orders on the machine. Ladle soup into bowls. Clean soup off underliners. Get yelled at by Skeet for making a mess of the soup area. Find cocktail sauce. Stand around with a ten-pound tray looking for a tray stand. Nearly drop tray. Consider bursting into tears. Back to the kitchen to find cooks screaming your name at the top of their lungs. Realize you've forgotten to pick up drinks. Tray up food. Return to grab lemon. Avoid meeting the eyes of the people whose drinks you'd totally forgotten. Slip on a piece of lettuce. Pick up drinks. Wrong drinks.

Return to bar. Pick up the right drinks. Answer questions from one table about where you were born while another table gives you death looks. Wait in line at the precheck while another new girl punches buttons randomly. Race to the kitchen, get yelled at by J.T. for not picking up orders. Definitely consider bursting into tears.

And suddenly it was over, and two hours had passed. The other waitresses were grinning and looking like the team that had won the Super Bowl. Everyone was drinking coffee and Pepsis. The smokers were sneaking forbidden cigarettes in the waitress station, waving the smoke away with menus.

Summer went to the kitchen. The cooks were cleaning up their stations and rocking out to Butthole Surfers.

Summer went to Skeet. "I'm sorry about messing up the soup," she said, practically sobbing.

Skeet looked amazed. "What?"

"And I'm sorry I didn't pick up my orders in time," Summer told J.T.

The cooks exchanged a look. Skeet said, "Aww, isn't that sweet? J.T., you a-hole, you got her all upset."

J.T. laughed, but not unkindly. "Come here." He motioned her down to the end of the line. He leaned back against the walk-in refrigerator door and sucked on a huge iced tea. His white uniform was stained and greasy. But he had nice, light brown hair pulled back in a ponytail and an open, somewhat lopsided smile. Summer could see why Marquez had been attracted to him.

"Summer," he said, "you don't pay attention to what we all say when we're in the weeds. When we're weeded, we get cranky. We have to yell at someone, and the waitresses are the traditional people to abuse."

"Oh. Who do *we* get to abuse?"

J.T. laughed. "Right back at us. Now, Marquez, when she gets yelled at, she throws it right back. She can curse in two languages. Three sometimes." He wiped the sweat from his forehead with a towel. "You did all right today, especially for it being only your second day."

"Thanks. I was kind of panicky, really."

He looked at her thoughtfully. "So I guess you and Marquez are hanging around together, huh?"

"Yeah, I guess so. I really like her."

He nodded and glanced across the room toward the dining room door. "I guess she told you about us?"

Summer tilted her head back and forth, an admission.

"Hope she didn't tell you too much bad stuff. How is she, anyway?"

"Marquez? She's great, I guess. She's the most totally unique person I've ever met."

His blue eyes were soft. "Yes, she is." He laughed. "Have you seen her room yet?"

"Isn't it great?"

"She's created that room, and she thinks she's going to be a lawyer someday," J.T. said. "My name used to be up on her wall, bigger than anyone's."

"It still is. I saw it."

He stood away from the walk-in. "It is? *My* name? I was sure she'd have painted it over."

"She said that's how it is, that she never paints over something."

J.T. shook his head in amazement. "When she broke up with this guy named Juan, his name was gone under three coats of white enamel before he managed to walk home." His eyes were bright. "J.T., right?"

"Big red letters," Summer confirmed.

Skeet yelled something rude, suggesting that J.T. might want to help do some of the work. "I gotta get back. Just remember, don't be sensitive around here. No one else is."

Summer saluted solemnly. "No more sensitivity. Absolutely."

Marquez was waiting for her as soon as she passed through the swinging doors to the dining room. She gave Summer a look and seemed about to ask a question, but stopped herself.

Summer suppressed a grin. Marquez wanted to know what she'd been discussing with J.T. That was obvious. And she didn't want to have to ask. Well, too bad. She'd just see how long Marquez could hold out.

"What's my side work?" Summer asked innocently.

Marquez glared at her through narrowed eyes. "You have sauces with me."

They dragged big plastic jars of cocktail sauce and tartar sauce out of the walk-in to the waitress station, where they stood side by side dumping spoonfuls of each into small dishes.

"So. Tonight's the big night," Marquez said. "You and Adam."

"Uh-huh. Actually . . ." Summer paused and looked around guiltily. Lianne was nowhere in sight. "Actually, after we do the beach thing I have to go run an errand with Seth." She said it as casually as she could.

Marquez was nowhere near being fooled. "An *errand*. She's running an *errand* with Mr. Moon. Did that picture of Diana's have anything to do with this?" Marquez giggled gleefully.

"Why did I even tell you?" Summer fumed. She slopped more tartar sauce. "It's not that, just for your information.

It's—" Again she looked over her shoulder. No Lianne. Summer lowered her voice. "Look, remember at Diana's how I said there was this guy—"

"—that spent the night with you! That was *Seth*?"

"No, no. Keep it down, Marquez."

"The kiss! The guy you kissed in a Laundromat who you didn't even know."

"It wasn't a Laundromat. It was a photo booth. At the airport." Summer sighed. There. She had told someone.

"How was it?" Marquez asked.

"The point is, Mar-*quez,* that I am just going with him to buy some tile this evening, after we go to the beach. That's all. I'm meeting him at his house."

"After we go to the beach and *before* you go out

tonight with Adam. Summer, Summer, Summer. I used to think you were such a nice, sweet girl." Marquez laughed. "I have to work a double shift, but I am coming over tonight after your date to get the complete story. So be prepared. This is not gossip that can wait."

Summer was feeling sort of pleased with herself, enjoying her new image as maybe-*not*-totally-nice, when Lianne came around the corner into the waitress station. She seemed to have appeared out of nowhere.

"Hi, you two," Lianne said. "Did I hear something about gossip?"

"This is my first time actually lying out in the sun," Summer said. "I figured when I came here I'd be spending every minute out on the beach. Look at me, I'm still white as snow." Summer adjusted her top and pried open one eye. Even through the sunglasses, as dark as she could find, the sun was still too intense. Her skin was hot on her exposed front, her back only slightly cooler on the towel laid out over sand the color of powdered sugar.

"Everyone thinks that," Marquez said, her voice slurred with sun sleep. Her reply came about two minutes late, as if the words had taken a long time to get to Summer, lying just a foot away. "I mean, when you're here on vacation, sure. But when you live here, you have other stuff to do. Like work."

Several minutes later Summer said, "Yeah."

The beach spread down the western edge of

Crab Claw Key, facing the Gulf of Mexico. The water was pure, translucent green, and as warm as the air. Summer had gone in up to her knees, and now there was sand stuck to her calves. The rest of her was coated with Hawaiian Tropic.

"How does sunscreen work?" Summer asked. No answer. "I mean, how does it keep . . . light. How does it keep sunlight from . . ." She couldn't think of the word. No point in wearing herself out thinking.

"Penetrating?" Marquez said eventually.

"Huh?"

"Penetrating. That's the word you wanted."

"Okay." Summer heard Marquez rolling over. She rolled over herself. They were pointed with their heads toward the water, the theory being that they didn't want to sunburn the bottoms of their feet as the sun crossed the line from east to west.

Summer opened her eyes again and looked out across the water. Far in the distance pillars of clouds rose, looking like fantastic islands of snow-covered peaks. It reminded her of watching the sunrise with Diver that morning.

Sunrise with Diver. Sunset would be with Adam. And in between, a little quality time with Seth. This vacation would be working out great if she could just lie back and enjoy it.

She must have been smiling, because Marquez said, "What's that grin all about? That looked lecherous."

"No, not lecherous," Summer said.

"Adam?"

Summer made a "maybe" look.

"Seth?"

"We're just shopping for floor tile."

"Uh-huh. You know, you two just look right for each other," Marquez said. "Like you could get married someday and have a bunch of wholesome children and a minivan."

Summer made a face. "That's how you see me, huh? A mommy with a bunch of kids?"

"Don't get pissed off," Marquez said. "It's just that he's a nice guy—not to mention the godlike body—and you're a nice girl. Nice in a good way."

"Maybe I don't want to end up with a nice guy," Summer said.

"Maybe you'd like a certain cute, very rich guy?" Marquez suggested.

"Maybe," Summer said, drawling the word and wiggling her eyebrows in a parody of seductiveness. "Did I tell you about the woman on the plane? The woman who did tarot cards? She told me I was going to meet three guys."

Marquez looked interested. "I don't believe in any of that superstitious junk."

"Me neither."

"So? What did she say?"

"She said I'd meet three guys here. One would seem to be a mystery, one would seem to be dangerous, and one would seem right."

"*Seem?* That's kind of weasely, isn't it?" Marquez asked. But she was looking thoughtful.

"So far you've met Adam and Seth, right? Are they supposed to be two of the guys?"

"How am I supposed to know? Maybe. Not that I believe any of that stuff. I mean, cards? Puh-leeze."

"You excited about seeing Adam tonight?" Marquez asked.

"As long as I can get a totally perfect tan between now and then I'll be happy." Summer twisted her head around to try and see the back of her legs. They looked pretty white. She was still an official chalk person.

"Where's he taking you? Somewhere *dangerous*? Somewhere *mysterious*? Or somewhere just *right*?"

Summer shrugged. "I don't know. He didn't say. I asked and he said just to leave it to him."

"Oh, the mighty macho man in control," Marquez mocked.

Summer flicked sand at Marquez. "That kind of reminds me of something. Guess who I talked to."

"Do I care?"

"I think you will," Summer said cockily. "I think you've been wanting to ask me all afternoon."

"I saw you," Marquez said, sounding utterly bored. She pretended to yawn. "I saw you talking to J.T. I was wondering if you were going to bring it up."

"He seemed very interested in *you*," Summer said.

Marquez sighed dramatically. "Okay, you might as well tell me what he had to say."

"I wouldn't want to bore you. I can tell you're not really interested."

Marquez pointed. "See that guy down there?

The big hairy old guy? If you don't tell me exactly what J.T. said, I'm going to tell that guy you're hot for him."

Summer related the conversation with J.T. as accurately as she could.

When she was done, Marquez slapped Summer's arm. "You weren't supposed to tell him his name was still on my wall."

"Oww. Why not?"

"He'll think I still like him."

"Do you?"

"Duh. I'll tell you one thing—he'd better not be your third tarot card."

"He's cute," Summer said. "But you know how sometimes a guy will be cute, but you don't react in *that* way?"

"No. Absolutely not. Okay, sure, I know what you mean."

"J.T. *is* cute, though," Summer repeated. "And he seemed nice."

"Yeah. He is cute. And he knows it. He has that Anglo, Nordic, blue-eyed thing going for him. Also, he's excellent at kissing. The creep. The subhuman." Marquez pounded the sand, but not so much in anger as in frustration. "He reminds me of you that way."

"What, you mean *I'm* a subhuman? Or has someone told you I'm excellent at kissing?"

Marquez laughed. "No, I mean the blue-eyed Nordic midwestern guy or girl next door thing. Speaking of which, we'd better get out of here before you get burned." Marquez stood up and began brushing sand off her stomach.

"So how come you and J.T. don't just make up?" Summer asked.

Marquez gave her a look that was cold as ice. "Because no guy ever gets to treat me like crap twice. Once. That's the limit. I don't hang with people who mess me up. I have more important things in my life, you know?"

The look surprised Summer. "More important than true love?"

"It isn't about what happens *now*, Summer. I'm just having fun now, but my life is about succeeding and making something out of myself and making my parents and my brothers proud of me. I'm not going to waste my mental energy dealing with jerks."

Summer stood looking at her.

"Sorry," Marquez said, rolling her eyes. "Sometimes I get this sudden attack of seriousness." She pointed up the beach. "See that point there? Up by the rocks?"

"Sure."

"That's the spot where my parents and my big brothers and little tiny Maria Marquez landed in this country." Marquez measured with her hands how tall she was at the time. "My dad was three years in prison in Cuba for complaining about the government. When he got out, we left. We were in a rowboat at night, and a Cuban navy patrol boat passed by only about a hundred yards away. If they'd spotted us, my dad and mom would have been thrown into prison and all us kids would have been taken away from them. We got blown around in the sea. I mean, I can still remember it a little. My mom was trying to act like it was this big family picnic, right? So, eventually we bang right into good old Crab Claw Key in the good old USA. We had the clothes we were wearing. That's it. No money. My dad and mom couldn't speak any English. Now my dad owns the gas station." She made a self-deprecating face. "Big deal, right? A gas station."

"Yes, a big deal," Summer said softly.

"He loves it, I can tell you that. You'd think that one gas station was the whole Shell Oil Company."

They began to cross the beach, feet sinking in the burning sand.

"Well, anyway, the thing is that I have to do better. Better than a gas station."

Summer gave her a quizzical, skeptical look. "Wait, so you can't forgive J.T. because you have to succeed?"

"That's right," Marquez said firmly. Then she made a sly grin. "You know, unless he begs. And crawls." She nodded thoughtfully. "Crawling would be good."

19

Finally—the Naked Truth

*L*ianne Greene watched from cool, air-conditioned comfort as Summer and Marquez made their way across the beach and paused at the low seawall to brush the sand from their legs.

She sat in the window of a small café, sipping an iced tea with mint. A raucous, Spanish-language game show was playing on the TV over the bar. Lianne had been there since the girls had arrived at the beach, having followed them from work to Marquez's house and then to the beach. She didn't mind waiting. It was boring, but she knew the next act in the little drama would make up for the long, dull wait.

Lianne left two dollars on the table and went outside. The heat seldom bothered her the way it did so many other people. It was all a trick of the mind, she believed. Stay calm and cool inside, and the sun couldn't reach you.

She followed Summer and Marquez at a safe distance, not that they would have noticed her had they turned around. She was wearing big sunglasses and a white cap with the bill low over her forehead.

Several times Summer and Marquez would stop just to laugh or playfully slap at each other. They were having a fine time. Especially Summer. And why shouldn't she be? She was on her way to pick up Seth.

A little knot of rage burned in Lianne's stomach. Seth was just a fool to fall for a girl like that. But then, that was Seth all over. He was too kind and decent to realize how people used him. He was too sweet to understand what a two-faced little manipulator Summer Smith was. And it was so obvious. Lianne had recognized her type right from the start.

They stopped at Marquez's house again, presumably so Summer could change clothes. Good. Lianne had plenty of time.

She knew Seth's house, inside and out. And she knew Seth better than anyone. That would make it all work. Then it would be bye-bye Summer.

And Seth would be right back where he belonged. Right where he would stay.

With her.

At four in the afternoon, the sun was still high and hot. The same clouds Summer had watched from the beach were darkening and building up over the water, threatening an afternoon thunderstorm.

Summer had showered quickly at Marquez's house and changed clothes. Marquez had turned up her nose at the top Summer was wearing and convinced her to borrow one of hers instead. Now Summer was walking across Seth's lawn, feeling conspicuous and worried that she was sending a message Seth might easily misinterpret.

"Yes," Summer muttered under her breath, tugging at the tight top, "this is how I always dress when I go to hardware stores."

Seth's grandfather's house was a low, flat-roofed bungalow, dwarfed by massive shade trees on all sides. One was a banyan, a tree that fascinated Summer. It looked like something from another planet, but its leaves defeated the sun and spread a welcome coolness.

There was a screened porch that went around two sides of the house. The screening was old and nearly opaque in the shade.

Summer was confused. There was a regular door on the left side and the screen door on the right. Which was the front door?

Then she heard a sound, the creak of springs, as if someone was sitting down in an old chair. The sound came from the porch. Summer headed toward the porch, still feeling ridiculous in the gaudy top Marquez had loaned her. Still feeling a quaking in her stomach, a feeling of uncertainty mingled with anticipation.

"Seth?" she said as she neared the screen door. No answer.

She climbed three stairs to the door. She cupped her hands around her face and pressed her nose against the screen to see inside. There was a rocking chair. Laid across the rocker, a pair of men's jeans. And over the jeans, Summer saw a white lace bra.

Close against the wall of the house, there was a bed. The bed wasn't empty.

"Oh, my gosh!" a female voice yelped. "Summer! What are you doing here?"

Lianne leapt up from the bed, snatching thin covers around her bare shoulders.

Summer could only gape, openmouthed.

"What are you doing here?" Lianne demanded again.

From inside the house, Seth's voice. "Lianne? *Lianne?*"

Summer stumbled back down the steps. "Sorry. I'm really, really sorry." She turned and ran as fast as she could back to the road.

Summer was nearly home by the time Seth caught up with her. She had been walking fast. Very fast.

She noticed him when he was still several blocks behind, trotting along in her wake, dodging the occasional car. He called to her to wait, but she continued doggedly. She was dangerously near tears.

They were both panting when she felt his hand

seize her arm. "Leave me alone," she snapped, shaking him off.

He fell in step beside her. "Look, Summer, that was not what it looked like."

"No? You mean that wasn't Lianne, lying in your bed when you knew I was coming over?" Summer wished she didn't sound so much like she cared.

"Will you hold up a minute? You're practically running."

"Go away."

"Come on, Summer, you at least owe me a chance to explain," Seth said angrily.

"Explain what? Why should you explain? You tell me it's over with Lianne, and then, whoops! Surprise! She's in your bed. While her clothes are not. No, her clothes are over with your clothes on the chair. What happened, you got up to get a drink?"

"Summer, this whole **thing** is just a setup. Lianne can't accept the fact that it's over," Seth said.

"You can't accept the fact that it's not," Summer shot back.

"That was low," Seth said.

"Don't tell me what's low," Summer muttered. Diana's house was just ahead. She raced up the driveway, around the side of the main house, down a narrow walkway lined with rosebushes.

Seth followed her, saying nothing while they were under the shadow of the main house. But out on the back lawn he exploded. "This is not fair, Summer. You have to give me a chance to explain."

"No. I don't."

"You *want* to be mad at me," Seth accused. "You want to believe what you think you saw is true so you can push me aside and go off with Richie Rich. Now you've had a good look at my house compared to Adam's house. I guess it's cooler to be going with a billionaire, huh?"

They had reached the walkway out to the stilt house. Suddenly Summer stopped and turned to face him. "This is my home, at least for now, and I don't want you in it. You can finish the work you have to do, but that's the end of our relationship."

She stomped several paces down the walkway, struggling to control her anger. She lost the struggle and turned again. "You talk about Adam's house and your house? The difference is that Adam doesn't have his girlfriend in his bed at the same time he's giving me all kinds of lines about . . . about air catching on fire and people being meant for each other."

Seth shook his head bitterly. "I was wrong about you. You're not so special."

"Jerk."

"Jerk."

"Go back to Lianne and leave me alone, you lowlife."

"Maybe I should," he said.

"Great, because I have better things to do. I have a date tonight."

"With Adam, I know."

"That's right, with Adam."

"Fine, go with Adam. I don't even care."

"Run home to Lianne, Seth. If you hurry, maybe you can get back *before she gets dressed*." The final shout echoed off the water.

This time Summer didn't turn back. She blew past Frank like a storm cloud, causing him to spread his wings and glide off toward a more peaceful perch.

20

Big Date, Big Questions,
and Diver for Dessert

The time Summer had allocated to be with Seth, to get to know him and to decide whether there was anything real between them, was spent instead on crying, storming around the house, wondering whether he was telling the truth somehow, and ultimately deciding to put him out of her mind for good.

By eight o'clock the swelling in her eyes had gone down with the help of two ice cubes. The anger was gone, too. It was all silly, she told herself. One of those things she'd look back on someday and laugh about. Ha ha. Seth wasn't the only guy in history to lie about having a girlfriend. He was a low, scum-sucking snake who masqueraded as a nice guy so he could seduce girls at the airport, but hey, Summer could handle it.

Ha ha ha. Just another jerk. He wouldn't be the

last she'd run into. But being cool—as she was—she'd just laugh it off. Ha ha.

She was dressed and ready and completely *not* angry anymore by the time she heard the engine of Adam's boat on the water outside.

Adam was standing at the wheel of the boat, its long prow nosed in under the stilt house as Summer descended slowly, a bit cautiously, through the hatch.

He had an almost dreamy smile on his face and was shaking his head admiringly. "That was a very nice start to the date," he said, offering his hand to help her aboard.

"What was?" she said, with just a trace of a snap in her tone.

"Watching you come down the stairs. Like an angel descending from heaven to visit earth."

"White as an angel, anyway," Summer said, blushing in a mixture of pleasure and embarrassment.

She stumbled a bit as the boat rolled. Adam caught her easily. He kissed her, just a playful kiss on the forehead. Then the playfulness went out of his eyes, and he kissed her lips.

Summer gasped when he pulled away.

"I've been wanting to do that since the other night," Adam said. "I've been thinking of nothing else."

"Sure, right," Summer said. It had been a very nice kiss. She would have enjoyed it even more if she hadn't still had half her mind on Seth.

"Cross my heart," Adam said. "This morning I

woke up thinking of you. I was imagining you here, in this house, warm and cozy in your bed. By the way, what *do* you wear to bed, just so I can be sure I had the picture right in my mind?"

"At home in Minnesota I wear a flannel shirt I got from my dad. And socks."

Adam grinned and gunned the engine a little, backing the boat away from the house. "I wasn't picturing you in Minnesota."

He steered the boat toward the open sea. Even at eight o'clock the sun was still bright, though it hung within inches of the horizon. "I guess you don't want to know what *I* wear to bed, huh?" Adam asked.

"Not especially."

"Pajamas with feet in them. And the little flap in back." He said it with such absolute sincerity that for a moment she believed it.

"Uh-huh. Right."

Summer drew a deep, steadying breath. Wait a minute, she told herself, she was letting Seth ruin her time with Adam. And that was stupid. She slid her hand into his as he opened the throttle. He squeezed her hand.

They motored clear around the circumference of Crab Claw Key, rounding the old side point, following the line of beach where Summer had sunned that afternoon with Marquez, gliding under the causeway, past the marshy, uninhabited north end of the island.

"What's all that white stuff in the trees over there?" Summer asked.

Adam turned the boat closer to land, and Summer could see that the "white stuff" was actually dozens, maybe even hundreds of wood storks. The birds seemed too large to be resting in trees, but there they were, looking like snow where no snow had ever fallen.

Slowly the last thoughts of Seth really did fade away, perhaps some effect of water and salt breezes. It was amazing how quickly every problem that existed on land seemed to evaporate, how alien the land seemed as they rode over gentle waves. It was as if the land were just some curiosity, a zoo filled with familiar creatures in familiar cages of stucco and wood.

From the sea, the interesting parts of the land weren't the things made by people, but the trees—tall, pencil-thin palms that swayed on the slightest breeze; stunning trees that were an explosion of garish red or lavender flowers; mangroves that grew right from the edge of the water.

They rounded the north end and again passed under the causeway, now cruising south along the new side's outer shore. This shore was lined with a mix of fantastically large new homes and smaller, humbler bungalows. Then the homes stopped abruptly and gave way to manicured grass and perfectly formed oaks fronting a stretch of pristine beach.

"This is the beginning of the estate," Adam said.

"Does it ever seem weird to you having all this land and this monster house?" Summer asked.

"I guess not. I guess it would seem weird to me

if I just had a normal house. You get used to what you know."

"Must be nice," Summer said. "Everything always perfect and beautiful."

"Not *always* perfect," Adam said. "Even rich people have problems."

Summer laughed. "Sure. Look at the Quartermaines."

"Who?"

"They're the rich family on *General Hospital*. Divorces, murders, evil twins, all kinds of problems."

"We haven't had any murders yet," Adam said dryly. He looked at Summer closely. "What did Diana tell you about me?"

"Nothing," Summer said. "Diana and I don't talk all that much. I think she's— Never mind."

"What? What were you going to say?"

"Just that she seems very sad to me. I'm probably wrong. Even Marquez says Diana always used to be a little antisocial but that she's gotten a lot worse. But I guess you know her a lot better than I do."

"I don't think she's gotten any worse," Adam said shortly. He was twisting the wheel in his hands. "I think she's the same as always. She was always a little different."

"It's like you can't quite communicate with her," Summer said. "Like you reach out to her, but she's never exactly there."

"Whatever it is, she'll get over it," Adam snapped. Then he forced a smile. "Let's not talk about old girlfriends or old boyfriends."

"I don't have any old boyfriends," Summer said.

"Maybe that's about to change," Adam said. The usual cocky yet self-mocking grin was back.

The boat rounded the point and entered the bay again, sidling up to the Merrick estate dock. Summer glanced across the water. The little stilt house stood out quite clearly, as did Diana's house.

"Thanks for the ride," Summer said as she climbed over to the dock.

"Anything in particular you'd like to do now?" Adam asked.

Summer shrugged. "Whatever you want."

"I wanted to check first because I didn't want to just be taking charge," he said.

"That's okay. If there's anything I don't want to do, I'll tell you," Summer said. She was feeling mellow to the point of dopiness after the boat trip.

"Well, I was just going to do some horseback riding, have dinner, watch a movie . . ."

"Wow."

He looked doubtful. "Too much for a first date? Does it look too much like I'm trying to impress you? At least I decided against trying to get the use of the helicopter to take you to a club in Miami."

"Now, that would have been too much," Summer agreed. "I don't have the clothes for a club."

"But how about the rest? Have you ever ridden a horse?"

"A horse?" Marquez asked, curling her lip in disgust. "*Have* you ever ridden a horse?" She took another of Summer's potato chips and crunched it noisily. She was still wearing her work uniform, having come straight over from finishing her dinner shift.

"I told him I hadn't," Summer said. "I wanted to make him tell me all this stuff about how to ride and all. Then I showed him." Summer giggled at the memory of Adam's face.

"Showed him what?"

"I started riding when I was like six years old," Summer said. "My grandmother owns a stable outside of Owatonna. That's a town in Minnesota," she added, noting the blank look on her friend's face.

"Of course. Who hasn't heard of Owatonna?"

"Anyway, it was good to be better than him at something. He's so sure of himself."

"So you rode, then what?"

"We had dinner. It was amazing. We had a picnic in this tower they have with windows all around, where you can see everything. We ate all this cool stuff that their cook made up. Little tiny sandwiches and shrimps and dessert."

Marquez crunched another chip. "Are you going to get to the good part? I just got done waiting on about a thousand tables. I don't want to hear about food."

"That *was* the good part. We had all this excellent food and watched the sun go down, only there weren't enough clouds to make a really excellent sunset."

Marquez looked shocked. "What? The Merrick family can't control the sunset?"

Summer sent her a pitying look. "Envy is so beneath you, Marquez."

"Come on, let's get on with the story. I didn't come all the way over here at practically midnight to hear *this* stuff."

"So then we watched a movie in their theater. Their own theater, with a projector and a screen and a popcorn machine."

"What movie?"

"That new Ethan Hawke movie."

Marquez closed her eyes and let her head float back and forth dreamily. "Ethan Hawke. That boy could get his name on my wall in very, very big letters."

Summer shifted uncomfortably on her bed. "Then we made out a little."

"How little?"

"A lot."

"Oh, a *lot* little." Marquez leaned close. "Okay. How was it?"

"It was excellent and fantastic, and I was scared because it was like if he'd tried to do anything more I don't know what I would have said, all right? It was like, so *much,* you know? The boat and the horses and the food and this romantic movie . . ."

"You were seized by the moment," Marquez said eagerly. "You were caught up, overwhelmed, carried away!"

"I wasn't carried away," Summer said. "I maybe could have been carried, though." She shook her head and rolled her shoulders to get rid of some tension. "I guess it's like Seth was saying about people coming here and losing their minds. I think I'm losing mine."

"So you're falling big time for Richie Rich, huh?"

Summer jumped up and walked nervously across the room. "I don't know, Marquez. Yes. Maybe. I mean, when I was with Adam, the answer was yes, definitely."

And when I'm with Diver . . . and with Seth, even though he's a toad . . .

"Well, you could do worse. Adam is major *A*-list material. He's beyond *A*-list. But speaking of which, what about Seth? Did you guys go to the hardware store?"

Summer told Marquez what had happened that afternoon. Marquez reacted with exactly as much sensitivity as Summer expected—she let out a loud whoop of delight.

"Oh, man, why don't things like this ever happen to me?" Marquez wailed.

"It wasn't exactly a good time, Marquez," Summer said.

"Not a *good* time, no," Marquez allowed. "But so extreme! Who'd have ever figured Mr. Moon was so twisted?"

"He hides a lot behind that innocent, midwestern face," Summer said darkly.

"Unless he's telling the truth," Marquez said.

"Oh, puh-leeeze."

"I'm just saying, it could be." Marquez shrugged.

"How do you figure that?" Summer pressed.

"Does it matter? Don't be worrying about two guys at once, Summer. One guy is already too many. Two is *way* too many."

How about three? Summer couldn't help adding silently.

She turned things over in her mind, biting an uneven fingernail. It was possible Seth was telling the truth, she supposed. Just barely, slightly possible.

"It's not *my* fault," Summer said at last. "I just don't know what to do. I mean, Adam, Seth . . ." Diver, she added silently. "How are you supposed to know?" Summer said. "How are you supposed to figure out the truth? How do you know if guys are interested in you or not? And how are you supposed to know if you really like them? How do you know if it's real?"

"I don't know," Marquez admitted. "I guess you should go out with both of them and see how you feel."

"What if one of them won't even go out with you?" Summer asked, voicing the question before she'd thought about it.

"Seth won't go out with you? Sure he will. Don't be stupid." Marquez stopped. "Wait a minute. Are you telling me there's a *third* guy? You're not, are you, because I can't take any more complications."

Suddenly, to Summer's horror, the hatch in the floor began to open.

Diver's head appeared. "Um, hi. I didn't want to interrupt when you have people over," he told

Summer. "But I'm really thirsty. Maybe I could just get a drink of water and then I'll bail."

Summer froze. Marquez froze with her mouth wide open. Only her eyes moved, going from Summer to Diver and back again.

"You might as well come in, Diver," Summer said. She covered her face with her hands. Why had she for a moment believed Diver would be able to keep himself a secret?

"Just a drink and I'm outta here. Hi," Diver said to Marquez.

For once Marquez seemed to have nothing to say. Diver cupped water from the sink faucet. He grabbed a soda from the refrigerator. Then, with a last wave, he disappeared back down the hatch.

At last Marquez found her voice. "Summer, Summer, Summer. I am really glad I met you, girl. I have a feeling nothing is going to be boring as long as you're here."

21

H i, Jennifer. Here I am again.

I was going to use the video camera to make this diary into kind of a cool documentary, you know? Like Winona Ryder in *Reality Bites*? But as you can see, it's just me again. Hi. It's dark because I don't want to turn on the light because Diver's outside on the roof and he might see it. Which is also why I'm whispering.

My life is such a mess. I mean, it's a good kind of mess. It's just very confusing. I guess it's better to have three guys to worry about rather than none, which is how many I had before I got here. It's like God suddenly realized I'd managed to get through my whole life without very many romantic problems and decided to make up for it all at once.

I went out with Adam tonight. You would not believe it, Jen. It's too dark for you to see my face, but I have this silly grin on it because it was this totally excellent evening.

But right before I left, I had this huge dumb fight with Seth. So, even while I was with Adam, sometimes even *while* Adam was kissing me, I would be thinking about Seth. Or other times Diver would suddenly pop into my head.

What is going on with me? You know me better than anyone. I'm just me. Normal old me. This is too much.

I asked Marquez about it, you know, how you can tell who is the *right* guy? I figured she would know because she had this long-term one-on-one thing with this guy named J.T. But that's when Diver poked his head through the floor and that was the end of *that* conversation.

So, I'm sitting here, whispering like an idiot, talking to a little black camera with a stupid blinking red light on it, trying to figure things out. How can I feel so . . . so wonderful when I'm with Adam. And at the same time be feeling mad and guilty because of Seth. And at the same time wondering, "Hmmm, I wonder if Diver has a real name, and I wonder if he ever wears real clothes?" It doesn't make sense, does it?

Aaargh! This is so confusing. Why aren't you here to straighten me out? You always know everything.

All I know is that this vacation is working out very differently than I expected. It's like I got on the plane at the airport *there,* normal Summer Smith, and by the time I stepped off the plane *here* I was someone different. Like not only did the place change, but I changed too.

Maybe that's the way it always is, Jen. Maybe when I'm in Bloomington, I'm part of Bloomington. And when I came here, I had to be part of this island.

Or maybe I'm just this wispy little wimp who gets blown back and forth depending on who I happen to be with.

Or maybe everyone there in Bloomington is just so used to me being a certain way that I was *already* different, only no one there noticed. See?

I know what you're saying, Jen. You're saying, "Summer, shut up already, you're giving me a headache. Quit all your whining and just go for it, girl."

That's easy for you to say. You're more experienced than I am. Maybe I'm just emotionally retarded. Remember how you got your period six months before I did? Maybe I'm just slow at everything.

Shhhheeeeesh. Ghaaaarrrr. Aaaaaaaargh.

There, I feel better now. I'll send this tape off so you can see just how insane your best friend has become.

22

All About Deep Holes and Cold Hearts

Diana woke in the hole.

It happened sometimes. Sometimes not. But she could always tell, as soon as her eyes opened.

The hole was blackness inside of blackness. It was a place where no light entered. It was a place of dull, relentless pain.

It happened sometimes. She wished she knew why. Why one day she felt okay, and the next she felt hopeless. The night before she had watched from her balcony as Adam had driven Summer away in his boat. And returned her hours later.

But that wasn't why she was in the hole. She wasn't jealous. Jealousy was too active an emotion to exist in the hole. There had been another emotion from watching Summer with Adam—a sense of loss, a realization that Diana had once been . . . *happy?*

Maybe not happy. Certainly not for a long time.

She kicked at the sheet that covered her, but it just tangled around her legs. She didn't want to get up, but she had to pee. Peeing right there in the bed was a bad idea. She would have to get up. Eventually.

If she just stopped eating and drinking, she could lie there without having to get up. If she did that, though, she'd die.

Yes.

After a while she got up and slumped toward her bathroom.

She saw herself in the mirror and leaned close, closer, till the outlines of her face blurred and all she could see there was the reflection of her own eyes. Eyes looking at eyes looking at eyes.

"Hi, there," she said to the reflection. "Having a good time? No? You're in the hole today? Me too."

Eyes looked at eyes looking at eyes.

"You're pathetic, you know that, right? Pathetic. You make everyone sick. You make *me* sick."

The eyes were crying now. Tears were welling and spilling, welling and spilling.

And Diana didn't care.

There was a knock.

"Go away," Diana whispered.

The knock came again. "Hey, Diana? Are you up?"

"Am I up?" Diana asked herself, viciously parodying Summer's chipper voice. "Am I up? No, I wouldn't say *up*."

"Diana? Are you on the phone? Can I come in? I just want to ask you something."

"I just want to ask you something," Diana muttered. "I just want to ask you something."

Now there was a knock much closer, louder. She was knocking on the bathroom door.

"Diana, are you okay?"

Concern now. Definite concern in Summer's voice. And just what the hell was little Summer going to do if cousin Diana wasn't okay?

"Go away," Diana said.

"Diana, are you all right?"

"I said go away. Leave me alone."

Silence. But not the sound of a person walking away.

"Look, Diana, I'm not going away till I'm sure you're all right."

Diana snatched at the door handle and threw it open. "Here I am, see?" Diana said. Her voice was guttural. "You happy now?"

Summer's eyes were wide with shock. There was fear there, too.

"Get out," Diana snapped. "Just get out. Go away."

Summer didn't move.

Suddenly Diana emitted a short laugh. "Fine. Stand there. I don't care. This what you came to see, all the way from Cowtown, all the way from the biggest mall in the whole wide world, *Summer*? Great, now you've seen it, *Summer*. You can go tell my mother, 'Yes, Diana looks like she might be a little strange,' *Summer*."

"Diana, what's the matter?"

"What's the matter? What's the matter?" Diana

mimicked. Then her voice became low, almost sultry. "You want to know what's the matter? I'm in a big, deep hole, and no matter what I try, I can't get out."

"What are you talking about?"

Diana felt the energy drain out of her. Her shoulders sagged. She hung her head. She ran her fingers back through her lank hair.

"Diana?" Summer said. She reached and took one of Diana's hands.

Diana stared blankly at her own dark hand, held in a web of Summer's almost translucent white fingers.

"It's just PMS," Diana said. She managed to plaster on a false, shaky smile. "Sorry. I didn't mean to yell at you. I'm just not feeling all that great this morning."

Summer didn't look convinced. She kept her grip on Diana's hand, and Diana didn't have the will to pull away.

I would give anything to be you, Diana thought. To have those contented blue eyes, even now touched by concern. To be a creature of light and sun and hope.

"Are you upset over Adam?" Summer asked. "I mean, because I'm seeing him?"

It was almost funny. Another time it would have made Diana laugh. "I think I'll just go back to bed." She disengaged her hand.

"I really like him, but if it's hurting you . . ." Summer said.

Diana took a closer look at Summer. She was wearing her stupid waitress uniform. She must be on her way to work or else on her way back. "It's over with me and Adam," Diana said wearily.

"But you still care about him, don't you?"

"No."

"I don't believe you."

"I don't care what you believe." Diana walked to her bed and flopped facedown, arms at her side.

"I have to get to work," Summer said. "But I want you to tell me something before I go. I want you to tell me why you and Adam broke up."

Diana stared at the pillow an inch from her face. It was a color called salmon. Fish-colored pillow.

Summer came and sat beside her. "Tell me."

"Tell you?" Diana muttered. "Tell you. I'll tell you just one thing."

"What?"

Diana sat up, hunched over the pillow, hugging it to her. "Just remember you're nothing to any of them. Just remember that. You're nothing. Not to Adam Merrick, not his father, not his . . . any of them. You're less than nothing."

Summer looked disappointed. Her mouth was in a tight line. She stood up. "I don't know why you're so mad at me, Diana. And I don't know why you're so sad. If you won't tell me anything, how am I supposed to help?"

"You're not supposed to," Diana said. "You can't."

"I have to go to work." She headed for the door.

"Summer," Diana called suddenly.

Her cousin turned back, questioning.

Diana felt her throat clutching up. The panic

feeling was rising in her. Soon it would sweep over her. She tried to speak and nothing came out. She took a deep breath and tried again. Her voice belonged to someone else, but the words came out. "Look out for Ross," Diana said.

"The soup is conch chowder, and we have blackened redfish for the special, $10.95," J.T. said.

Marquez dutifully wrote this information down with a red dry marker on a white board.

"Make sure everyone knows we only have three lobsters. We didn't get the shipment today," J.T. added. He was standing behind the line in the kitchen, arms folded over his white cook's shirt.

"Anything else?" Marquez asked.

"You're so tough, aren't you?"

Marquez looked up from the board. She could feel the blood rushing to her face. "Excuse me?"

"I said you're real tough, real cold, Marquez."

"We are not going to do this here in front of everyone," Marquez said firmly.

"Walk in," J.T. said, pointing toward the walk-in refrigerator.

"This is work here," Marquez said. "You want to talk to me, maybe you should do it some other time."

"I've had almost two weeks of your attitude," J.T. said.

Marquez saw Summer come into the kitchen. Skeet was looking down at her work, pretending to be totally absorbed in wrapping bacon around shrimp.

Without a word Marquez stomped to the walk-in.

It was chilly inside and not exactly roomy as she stood between bins of chopped lettuce and shelves loaded with salad dressing, sliced vegetables, and trays of fish filets lined up in neat rows.

J.T. closed the walk-in door and stood there, glaring at her. "You didn't take my name off your wall."

"I haven't gotten around to it yet," Marquez said. "But if it bothers you, I'll make sure I paint over it this afternoon."

"Yeah, you would," he said.

"You're the one who started this, J.T.," Marquez pointed out. "Was it *me* saying I wanted to see other *guys*? No."

"I told you I was sorry about that. It was just something I said because I was upset." He straightened a tray of tomatoes. "I was freaked, and you were giving me nothing. As usual."

"Oh, and so I'm supposed to just forget it?"

"No, you're supposed to realize that I've been going through some stuff, all right?" he said.

"Why is that *my* problem?"

He rolled his eyes. "Why is it your problem? I don't know—maybe because you supposedly love me."

Marquez winced. She rubbed her bare upper arms. The cold was beginning to have an effect. "Look, J.T., I'm sorry, all right? I'm sorry you found out some stuff you weren't supposed to know. If it hadn't been for bad luck, you'd be happy and normal, right? Your mom would be your mom, your dad would be your dad. So why not just forget it? Lots of people are adopted."

"Man, Marquez, is that really the way you think? Are you really that cold?" He threw up his hands. "Of course you are. How stupid of me."

"Are you done? Because, speaking of cold, this *is* a refrigerator."

"I just wanted some sympathy, you know?" he pleaded. "I wanted you to be there for me."

"Yeah? When was I supposed to *be* there for you, J.T.? When you were throwing things around my room and yelling about how you were going to go find some other girl? How easy it would be for you to find someone else?"

"I told you, I was freaked. I was messed up. I needed some understanding from you, and I wasn't getting it, so what else was I going to say?"

"Great. Cool. No problem," Marquez said. "You want to talk a lot of crap, fine. Only don't expect me to take it."

J.T. was silent, hanging his head. He picked at a loose label on a jar of blue cheese dressing. Marquez shivered and stopped her teeth from chattering.

"There hasn't been anyone else," J.T. said. "You know that, right?"

"How would I know that?" Marquez said. But her anger had begun to ebb.

"Well, I'm telling you. There hasn't been anyone else." He looked at her with a question in his eyes.

"I haven't had time to be out picking up new guys," Marquez admitted.

His answer was a gentle wisp of a smile.

"J.T., you have to get over this now. Your parents

lied. It happens sometimes. They didn't lie in order to hurt you. You should be proud you're adopted. That means they had to really want you."

J.T. nodded. "I don't have a birth certificate," he said in a conversational tone. "I needed one to get a social security card, right? Last summer, when I first started here. So I asked my mom. She gets me down a baptism certificate instead. She says that will do just as well, and she was right, they accepted it."

"So?"

"So I was two and a half when I was baptized," J.T. said. "In our religion you get baptized when you're a few days old."

"Maybe your real mother, your birth mother, didn't baptize you and your mom and dad wanted to make sure."

He nodded. "Yeah, that's what I figured. But after I found out, you know, about all this, I checked. See, when you get adopted, they issue you a new birth certificate showing the names of the adoptive parents. It's like they rewrite the record, so that adopted kids have a birth certificate."

"Is there a point to this story? I have side work to do."

"The point is, why don't I have a birth certificate? Why isn't there a record of me until I was more than two years old?"

"I don't know," Marquez said impatiently.

J.T. nodded. "Sorry to lay it on you. I know you don't give a damn." He forced a grim, angry smile and threw open the walk-in door.

23

Marquez's Walls, Summer's Floor, and Adam's Many Bathrooms

T wenty-seven dollars even," Marquez said. She had the money arranged in neat stacks on the counter in her room: two fives, a number of singles, quarters, dimes, and nickels.

"Thirty-four dollars and forty cents," Summer reported. Her stack was mostly singles.

"You made more than me?" Marquez demanded. "On your first real day?"

"I guess so."

Marquez shrugged. "Well, I was in a lousy mood. People may have picked up on that."

"I wasn't in a great mood either," Summer said. "I told you about my little encounter with Lianne at work. She just kept apologizing, like it was all her fault, and *I'm* the one who was barging in on her."

Marquez gave a noncommittal nod.

"And the day started out even worse," Summer

said. "Diana yelled at me this morning before I went to work."

"Diana yelled?" Marquez asked sharply. "Why?"

"I don't know. She said it was PMS. But I think she may be messed up over something. I mean, *real* messed up."

Their eyes met. Summer could see that Marquez didn't dismiss this possibility.

"She shouldn't rag on you about it," Marquez said. "You bring a suit?"

"In my bag," Summer said. She began stripping off her uniform. "Maybe she had to take it out on someone. Her mom isn't around for her. She doesn't seem to have a lot of friends."

"That doesn't mean it's *your* problem,"

Summer was looking at her thoughtfully.

"What?" Marquez demanded.

"I'm wondering if Diana's PMS is catching."

Marquez rolled her eyes but laughed. "I guess you heard about me and J.T. playing rock-'em sock-'em robots in the walk-in."

Summer wasn't sure how to answer that question. The gossip machine at the restaurant worked at the speed of light. "Skeet may have mentioned something about it."

"Uh-huh. Skeet's your friend now, huh? Don't go leading her on."

"Very funny." Summer tied on her bathing suit top. She pulled the side of her suit bottom away for an inch, hoping to see some evidence that a tan line was developing. There was none.

"I can't believe how polite you are," Marquez said. "You aren't going to ask me what J.T. and I were fighting about?"

Summer batted her eyes. "I'm too polite."

"It was the same stuff. He did apologize for what he said about wanting to see other girls. He said it was because I wasn't supportive. Do you think I'm not supportive?"

"I don't really know you all that well, Marquez," Summer said, evading the question.

"Don't give me that. You don't think I'm supportive?" Marquez was standing with hands on hips, looking intense.

"I don't know about supportive. I know you kind of intimidate people. At least me you do. Not that you *try* to intimidate, it's just that you're so—"

"So *what?*"

"You're just so you. It's like you always know who you are and what you're doing. Some people aren't that sure, I guess. *I'm* not."

Marquez looked troubled. "I'm not *always* sure. Yeah, I know *who* I am, like you said, but everyone knows who they are."

"No, they don't," Summer said. "Lots of times I don't. Lots of times I'm like a cloud changing shapes with the wind. It's like people look at me and some think I look like a rabbit or a squirrel, and others think, no, that cloud looks like a map of Australia."

"Australia?"

Summer was beginning to feel foolish, but she wasn't going to be cowed. "I'm just saying, how do you know what you are or who you are? I've been thinking about it a lot lately."

Marquez didn't laugh. Instead her eyes drifted toward the big red letters that spelled out *J. T.*

"Like if you suddenly found out your parents weren't your parents," Marquez said. "I guess that could make you confused about who you are."

Summer decided against saying anything. She hadn't said what she'd said in order to make Marquez feel bad.

"Ready to go?" Marquez said, suddenly switching on her cheerful voice.

"Ready. I'm not going to get tan hanging around in here."

"Tourist." Marquez laughed. "Come on, we'll turn you nice and dark, little Minnesota person." They went outside into the blistering sun and started toward the beach.

"By the way," Marquez said, sounding a little too casual, "not to bring up unhappy things . . . I was just wondering, Summer. I mean . . . you have such a cool name and all. *Summer.* What was your brother's name? I know you told me already, but I wasn't sure. It wasn't *Winter,* I guess? Or *Spring.*"

"No, it was Jonathan," Summer said. Why did Marquez care?

"Jonathan," Marquez repeated the name slowly. "Jonathan. Pretty common name. Not like Summer."

"It is pretty common, yeah."

*   *   *

"Good evening, Frank. How's fishing?" Summer said when she arrived back at the stilt house. "I see you've started replacing the bird poop that was washed away."

Frank spread his wings, startling her.

"Just a joke," she said.

She opened the door of the house and gasped. The cheesy indoor/outdoor carpeting had been ripped up off the floor, which was now bare wood, studded with the protruding heads of nails. In the kitchen the linoleum was off the floor. It was off in the bathroom, too, revealing some unpleasant-looking wood subflooring. In one place she could look straight down through a crack widened by rot and see the water beneath the house.

She found the note from Seth resting on her table.

Summer:

Sorry to leave such a mess, but I wanted to get all the old linoleum up at once so we could just make one trip to the dump. Be back tomorrow to start laying the carpet and the tile. By the way, don't use the bathroom; the floor is too dangerous in here. You'd better use one in the big house.

Sorry. Right. *Right.* He had made a total mess of the place. A *total* mess. "Don't use the bathroom?" she muttered. It was hard not to suspect that Seth was being slightly spiteful. *Don't use the bathroom.* Oh, sure, no problem.

She crumpled the note and threw it at the wastebasket. She missed, so she kicked it and missed again, banging her toe into the table leg.

She was cursing Seth when there was a knock at the hatch in the floor.

"Who is it?" she snapped.

"Adam. But I'm not coming in if you sound like that."

She hobbled over to the hatch and raised it. "Sorry, I banged my toe." She must have been cursing too loudly to notice the boat's engine.

Adam stuck his head up through the floor and whistled. "Is Mr. Moon pissed at you or something?" He climbed the rest of the way up.

Summer tried to massage her toe and started to tip over. Adam grabbed her and steadied her. "You want me to kiss it and make it better?"

"My toe?" Summer laughed.

"How about this instead?" He wrapped his arms around her and kissed her, lightly once, and then, when she stopped holding her toe, more deeply.

"That helped," Summer said breathily.

"A definite mess," Adam said, releasing her. "Good thing I'm here to take you away from all this. I just stopped by to see if you had anything planned for tonight."

"We're going out tomorrow, I thought."

"Yeah, I know. But I couldn't wait till then to see you again."

"Really?" Summer asked, wanting to hear him say it again.

"Really. I was sitting around doing nothing, and I kept thinking 'There she is, just across the bay.'"

"I just got home myself," Summer said, feeling very pleased with herself. "Marquez and I went to the beach again, in search of the perfect tan. As you can see, I didn't get it."

"You don't need a perfect tan. You are perfect."

Summer felt warmth suffuse her body. But at the same time, she was acutely aware that she was wearing nothing but a bathing suit, and that his gaze was very attentive.

"I was, uh . . ." She completely forgot what she was going to say.

"Look, this place is trashed. Where are you going to stay tonight? You can't stay here."

"I guess I'll go barge in on Diana," Summer said. The thought wasn't pleasant. Diana wasn't exactly hospitable at the best of times. And judging by this morning, this was not the best of times. "She has all kinds of room there. I'd stay here, only Seth says I shouldn't go into the bathroom."

"That's certainly convenient. Just hold it till tomorrow. Look, I know a place with lots and lots of bathrooms," Adam said. Then, seeing her reaction, he hastened to add, "No, no, it's not what you think. We have guests staying there all the time. We had the ambassador of France and his wife there, we've even had a bishop stay there. No wife, of course. But if it's safe enough for a bishop . . ."

Summer could see a clear picture in her mind of Adam's house. And an even clearer picture of the mess that Seth had left her. "It wouldn't be like I was staying *with* you," Summer began. "I mean—"

"I *know* what you mean," Adam said. He pretended to be offended. "What kind of dog do you think I am?"

"Okay," Summer said dubiously. It gave her some pleasure to think how annoyed Seth would be that by tearing up her house she would end up sleeping at Adam's house. "Let me change and get my stuff. Which means you'd better wait down in your boat. I can't go into the bathroom to change."

"Yes, ma'am," Adam said.

As Summer quickly changed out of her suit, two thoughts struck her with sudden force:

1. She had to let Diver know about the bathroom floor situation. What if he fell through?

2. She was spending the night at a guy's house!

Her stomach did a quick turn. She hadn't thought this through. She had barely hesitated. What was the matter with her? Was she crazy?

She was about to tell Adam she had reconsidered but stopped herself. Why should she? Adam's house was as big as a hotel, wasn't it? It wasn't like they would be sharing a room. They would probably end up as far apart as two people at opposite ends of a football field.

"Are you coming?" Adam called up through the floor.

"Right there!" Summer yelled back.

Okay, a note to Diver. But where to leave it? On the floor by the hatch. That way he was sure to see it.

She grabbed a piece of paper and a felt-tip pen.

> Dear Diver,
> The place is a mess because Seth is supposedly fixing it, so you can't use the bathroom or you might fall through the floor. Be careful.

Now to sign it. Her pen was poised over the sheet. "Summer?" she asked herself. "Love, Summer?" No. Not love. He'd get the wrong idea. His *wa* might be disturbed.

"Sincerely?" Yeah, right. She'd said "dear." Not that it meant anything because that was how you always started a letter.

> Love, Summer

What if Diver didn't see the note, but Seth did when he came in the morning?

She shook her head. Marquez was right. She *was* in trouble.

She rested the note beside the hatchway. *Love, Summer* was just the same as *Dear Diver.* No biggie. Forget it. And staying at Adam's house was just like staying at a hotel. Also no biggie.

Oh, man.

24

Old Fear, New Passion,
and Diana's Sadness

*B*y the time the sun set and darkness fell, Diana was tired of her bed. She had been there from sunrise to sunset. And now, suddenly, a restless nervous energy was rattling her legs, making her feel twitchy.

She had to get out. The house was too quiet. Too big and empty.

She showered, scrubbing almost violently at skin tattooed by the pressure of crumpled sheets. She shampooed her hair and left it wet and combed straight back. She avoided looking at herself in the mirror and dressed with feverish haste.

She was in her car, sitting in the driveway with the engine running, before it occurred to her that she really had no place to go. The kids at the institute would all be in bed. Besides, volunteers were asked not to disrupt the comforting regularity of the schedule there. Too many of the kids associated any change in routine with something bad.

She had no friends. Not anymore. The stores were mostly closed.

She could drive down to Key West. There were plenty of restaurants open there, places where she wasn't likely to run into former friends.

She pulled out onto the road and headed toward town. Yes, some serious, speed-limit-busting highway driving. That's what she needed to burn off some of this manic energy. Maybe she should have taken Mallory's Mercedes. It was faster.

She was pulling through town when she saw him. She had stopped for the light. He was with two other guys, crossing the street, right in front of her.

Ross Merrick.

Diana stopped breathing. She'd guessed he was back in town. The six months in rehab had been up a while ago. The *second* six months in rehab.

Diana recognized the other two guys, both hangers-on, the kind of creeps who hung out at the fringes of the Merrick family, sucking up to Ross and Adam, looking for the free plane trips and meals and parties.

They were right in front of her. If he turned, he would see her.

Diana shrank behind the wheel. If only the light would change.

There was a muffled bang. Something had hit the car. Ross.

He turned slowly, eyes trying to focus.

The look sent a chill of terror through Diana. It was that same look. He was drunk. Drunk and with that same dangerous leer.

He waved her off, a bleary apology for staggering against her car. Then he stopped. He bent down to peer inside the car.

And then he grinned.

Their eyes met.

He looked at her and silently mouthed words that were all too easy to read.

The light turned green.

Ross and his toadies headed off down the street, hanging on to each other, swaggering and shouting into the night.

Diana gripped the wheel with white fingers. She waited there through the next cycle of the light, ignoring angry horns blowing behind her.

"It's catching fire!" Adam warned.

Summer pulled the marshmallow from the fire but let it burn till the outside was crispy black, caramelized all over. It hissed as it burned, louder even than the crackle of the fire.

She raised the straightened coat hanger and held the burning marshmallow against the black sky overhead. "Look, it's a comet," she said.

"Yeah, but now you can't eat it," Adam said. He was toasting his own marshmallow more carefully, trying to get it an even brown all the way around.

"This is just how I like them." Summer blew out the flaming marshmallow comet and gingerly drew it off the end of the hanger. She popped the whole sticky mess in her mouth.

"That's disgusting, you realize," Adam said. He pulled off his own marshmallow and scarfed it up.

"Itf perfek fis way," Summer mumbled.

"Mime is beher," Adam argued.

They were on the Merricks' private beach, a neatly groomed stretch of sand bordered by palm trees. A pair of Hobie Cats were pulled up on the sand nearby. Just down the beach was a cabana and a barbecue grill.

As usual the gulf was calm, lapping in a restrained way, soft crashing noises followed by the rattle of a million tiny shells. Each foamy curl came a little closer to their small bonfire.

Summer set her marshmallow stick aside and leaned back against Adam. He cradled her head on his lap and looked down at her with eyes that reflected the fire's light.

"This is just exactly the reason why I wanted to come here to Florida," Summer said.

"What? You don't have marshmallows in North Dakota?"

"You *know* it's Minnesota," Summer said complacently. "I meant this night. Stars and warm breeze and the sound of the water."

"And?"

"And the sand and the bonfire."

"And?" he insisted.

"Did I mention the stars?"

He playfully pushed her head away.

"Okay, okay," she said, giggling and reclaiming her warm spot on his lap. "I did leave out the best thing of all."

"Which is . . ."

"You know it's *you*," Summer said. "Although even in my best daydreams about how cool it would be, I didn't imagine you."

"You didn't expect to meet guys?"

Guys, plural, Summer thought. If only he knew. But she was putting that behind her. This was the time to feel very content to be here with Adam, to savor the way he looked at her, the hard muscles of his thigh under her neck, the way he rested his arm across her bare stomach.

She had made a decision. She'd made it without even knowing it. She couldn't look back and point to the exact time. Maybe it had been at the moment when she agreed to spend the night at his house. Maybe it had just happened a moment ago.

He wanted to kiss her, she was certain of that. And she wanted to kiss him. Yet neither of them had, since coming out to this perfect beach, and the tension over when they would was sweet and agonizing at the same time.

"How could I have expected to meet you?" Summer said, with wonder in her voice. "I didn't even know guys like you existed. All the other guys I ever knew were so dorky and immature compared with you." She grimaced. "*That* sounded dorky and immature, didn't it? I just meant that you're so different."

"That's because I'm really thirty," Adam said. "Didn't I mention that? People just think I'm eighteen."

"You like much younger girls, huh? What are you, some kind of perv?"

"I just like one younger girl," Adam said, and his voice was low with emotion.

He slipped his hand under her head and raised her slowly, ever so slowly, till her lips met his.

They kissed for what might have been minutes or hours. She felt his lips on hers, on her throat, on the back of her neck, making every hair on her head tingle. With his fingers he stroked her cheeks, and smoothed back her hair, and sometimes just touched her lips, as if he couldn't believe they were real.

Her mind was firing away, thoughts flying back across time and forward to some imagined future. And through it all, the realization that she was feeling things she had never before felt with such intensity. Pleasure and fear and guilt and anticipation and desire. And a new emotion that was some blending of them all.

Love? Was this love? Or was it an illusion woven together out of gentle touches and slowly dying fires and bright clouds scudding swiftly across the moon and infinitely sweet kisses?

She heard a loud hiss, and the firelight was gone. A second later the warm foam covered her feet.

"Oops, tide coming in," Adam said. "Stay here any longer and we'll get swept out to sea."

Summer sat up, reluctant to break the contact with him. Far out to sea there was a prolonged flash of lightning.

Adam helped her to her feet and took her in his arms again. "I guess we should go inside," he said. "If the tide doesn't get us, that storm out there will. It's blowing this way."

They walked slowly back to the house, following the beach, holding hands. Adam stopped at the cabana and hosed the sand off their feet.

"Manolo sees sand in the house, he threatens to quit," Adam explained. "Although he's off tonight, so I guess we could be brave and track in two or three grains."

They held hands and laughed quietly all the way to the house and down the long, gloomy hallway of dead ancestors.

"Aww, isn't that sweet?" A voice spoke from the darkness of the big common room. It was impossible to tell where it had come from in the maze of couches and chairs. The fireplace fire had been allowed to die down and was just embers now, like the fire they'd left on the beach.

Summer felt Adam's muscles stiffen as he squeezed her hand.

"Home early, aren't you, Ross?" Adam said.

Summer peered and could see a shadow. In this light he could have been Adam, the resemblance was so close.

"Bartender at the Pier actually had the guts to card me," Ross said. "So I came home to raid the domestic stock." He held up a glass. "Would you two lovebirds care to join me?"

"No, thanks," Adam said evenly.

Ross came closer, holding himself up by resting against a couch back. He peered at Summer. "Do I know you?"

"Summer Smith," Summer said. "We kind of met at the party."

"What party? Never mind. It's all the same party." He took a longer look and then glanced at Adam. "You do have good taste, little brother," he said.

Adam pulled Summer toward him. "Good night, Ross."

"Where are *you* going?"

"To show Summer her room. She's spending the night. Her house is having repairs done."

Ross started to say something, looked at his brother, and decided to take another drink.

"Come on, Summer," Adam said gently.

"Good night," Summer said to Ross.

Ross said nothing, but as she walked away, Summer could feel his eyes on her.

It would have been impossible at that moment not to see Diana's face in her mind's eye. A sad, haunted-looking Diana saying, "Look out for Ross."

Marquez was half asleep, staring blankly at Letterman's Top Ten list on the TV, when she jumped at the sound of something rapping at her window.

"Madre de Dios!"

She seldom spoke Spanish unless cursing. She climbed out of bed and pulled back the edge of the curtain that blocked off the big shop display window.

"Seth? Diana?" *Diana? Here?*

"Let us in," Seth said tersely.

Marquez let the curtain fall back. Midnight, and suddenly Diana shows up with Seth?

It had to be bad news of some kind. She dug around in a pile of clothes, found a bathrobe, and let them in. Both were soaked through, clothing clinging to their skin, hair matted.

Seth was hovering at Diana's side, too close, as if he were afraid for her. He kept glancing at her with worried, wary eyes, as if ready to spring to her side and prop her up.

But Diana didn't look as if she were going to fall. She was nearly vibrating with electric energy. She pushed past Marquez into the room, looking around with quick, jerky little bird movements.

"Good evening to you, too," Marquez said huffily. "You know it's midnight?"

"Is Summer here?"

"No. What would Summer be doing here?"

"Do you know where she is? I banged on her door for about an hour and she's not at home. I went in and I found a note on her floor."

"What note? What are you talking about?"

"I found Diana wandering around in the rain downtown," Seth said, speaking for the first time. "She said she was coming here, so I offered to take her."

"Is she high or something?" Marquez asked Seth in a quiet aside.

He shrugged.

Diana had stopped pacing and was staring at her own name on Marquez's wall. "We used to be friends, didn't we, Marquez?" she said.

"Did we?" Marquez asked archly.

Diana was unaffected by the sarcasm. Marquez had never seen this side of Diana. If it wasn't drugs, it was way too many cups of coffee.

"You know, I never wanted her to come here," Diana said. She was picking through the CDs on the counter.

"What?"

"Summer. I never wanted her to come here."

"I think we all kind of figured that out," Marquez said.

"It's not my job to take care of her," Diana said.

"Diana, why don't you sit down and tell me what's going on?"

"I'm wet. I don't want to get everything wet. I'll go. I just was wondering if Summer was here. You don't know where she is, do you?"

Marquez shrugged. "The only other person she knows around here is Adam."

"Who's the diver?" Diana asked suddenly.

"The diver?"

Diana shook a damp note in Marquez's face. "She wrote a note to some Diver person. Told him to be careful because Seth had torn up the place."

Seth winced.

"Seth tore up the place?" Marquez asked, arching an eyebrow at Seth.

"I had to take up the—" Seth began, but Diana cut him off.

"He's fixing her place, Marquez. Don't act stupid!"

Marquez would have been offended, would have lashed back, but there was something frightening in the way Diana was acting. She hesitated for only a moment. If she guessed wrong about Diana, then Summer was going to be mightily pissed. "Diver is a guy Summer knows."

"Maybe she's at *his* house, then," Diana said eagerly.

"No. He lives at the stilt house. He sort of lives with Summer."

"What?" Seth demanded.

Momentarily Diana snapped out of her frenzy. "She has a guy *living* with her? She just got here."

"It's a long story. Look, Diana, you're starting to scare me."

Diana waved her off impatiently. "Nothing to be scared of. I'm sure she'll be fine. I told her to look out for Ross. I mean, I did warn her."

Marquez had had enough. She grabbed Diana by her shoulders and forced her to sit down on the bed.

"I'll get it wet."

"Tell me, Diana. Why did you warn Summer about Ross Merrick?"

"He was supposed to be rehabbed," Diana said bitterly. "But I saw him, and he was drunk."

"He was drunk at the party the other night,

too," Marquez said impatiently. "What else is new?"

Diana was biting her knuckles. Marquez was afraid they would start to bleed. "I didn't know."

"Diana . . ."

"It's no big deal. He tried to rape me, is all, but he was drunk, and . . ." She faltered, unable to go on.

Marquez felt like the floor was moving. Like she might lose her balance and fall.

On the television, Letterman was interviewing Charles Grodin. Seth had turned to stone.

Diana had become very small, a tiny, shivering wet figure, lost in a vast room.

"Adam said I shouldn't make a big deal out of it. I mean . . . you know, the family and all. And there would be all this mess. Besides, you know, Ross was going to get help."

Diana dug her fingernails into her arms, clawing herself almost violently.

Marquez drew back instinctively. She looked for a place to go, to pull away. Her gaze fell on the big red letters. *J. T.*

She looked back, unwillingly, at Diana, lost and alone and so filled with self-loathing that it was like a force field vibrating the air around her.

Not my problem, Marquez told herself. *Not even close to being my problem.* But Seth was too stunned, too paralyzed to help. And Diana needed someone. Anyone.

Marquez walked back to the bed. She sat beside Diana and put her arm around her quaking shoulders.

25

What Summer Knew

A dam and Summer sat side by side on the floor of his room, talking in soft voices, kissing, sipping sodas, intermittently watching MTV and pretending to be Beavis and Butt-head commenting on each video.

Letterman was on when Summer started to yawn.

"Sleepy? I'd better show you your room," Adam said.

"Unless . . . It's such a long walk." He flinched, as if he were waiting for her to throw something at him.

Summer smiled and yawned again. "You'd better show me *my* room. No matter how long the walk is."

He held up his hands in surrender. "I had to try."

She took his hand and pulled him up off the bed. "Come on." She grabbed her bag and followed him down the corridor and around a corner.

He opened a door and reached in to flip on a light.

Summer groaned. "Look at this room! Oh, I could get used to this very easily."

"Your own bathroom right there." Adam pointed. "TV there, radio alarm clock. What else?" He looked around. "Oh, yes. Bed. Big, lonely, empty bed."

"Thank you," Summer said primly.

"Hey, where's my tip? I showed you to your room."

"Like *you* need me to give you money?" Summer said.

"Who said anything about money?" He put his arms around her and kissed her till she was gasping for air and feeling weak.

"I'll let you get some sleep," he said.

"Good night."

He turned away.

"Adam? It was a really beautiful evening. The stars, the ocean, the marshmallows."

"And?"

"And you," Summer said softly. "Definitely you."

He swallowed. "I am leaving this minute, and you might just want to lock your door after I'm gone. Because I don't know how long my decent impulses will last."

Summer laughed. "Get out of here."

When he was gone, she explored the room for a little while and washed her face. Her hair smelled of wood smoke and sea salt, but she decided she didn't want to wash that away, not yet.

She climbed into the bed and flipped on the

TV. Sleep overtook her quickly, even though moments before she had felt too excited to even think about falling asleep.

She dozed and woke just long enough to turn Letterman off.

She slept. For how long she didn't know. She slept and dreamed of things that brought a smile to her lips, of tarot cards and three guys. In her dream she knew which was which—the right one, the mystery, the wrong one. She knew the choice she would make, as if she could see far, far into the future, past many months and years. In her dream she laughed and said, "Oh, of course, it had to be you all along."

Summer awoke, aware of a noise. A soft, imperceptible noise. She opened her eyes and saw the door of her room opening.

Adam, silhouetted against soft light. He had come back. Maybe she *should* have locked her door. He sagged against the doorjamb, and in an instant Summer knew.

From far, far off there was a faint, insistent pounding noise.

About the Author

After Katherine Applegate graduated from college, she spent time waiting tables, typing (badly), watering plants, wandering randomly from one place to the next with her boyfriend, and just generally wasting her time. When she grew sufficiently tired of performing brain-dead minimum-wage work, she decided it was time to become a famous writer. Anyway, a writer. Writing proved to be an ideal career choice, as it involved neither physical exertion nor uncomfortable clothing, and required no social skills.

Ms. Applegate has written sixty books under her own name and a variety of pseudonyms. She has no children, is active in no organizations, and has never been invited to address a joint session of Congress. She does, however, have an evil, foot-biting cat named Dick, and she still enjoys wandering randomly from one place to the next with her boyfriend.

Summer

by Katherine Applegate

- ⭘ **June Dreams**   51030-4/$3.50
- ⭘ **July's Promise**   51031-2/$3.50
- ⭘ **August Magic**   51032-0/$3.99
- ⭘ **Spring Break Special Edition**
                          51041-x/$3.99
- ⭘ **Sand, Surf, and Secrets**
                          51037-1/$3.99
- ⭘ **Rays, Romance, and Rivalry**
                          51039-8/$3.99
- ⭘ **Boys, Beaches, and Betrayal**
                          51040-1/$3.99
- ⭘ **Special Christmas Edition**
                          51042-8/$3.99

Available from Archway Paperbacks